RAISING the BAR

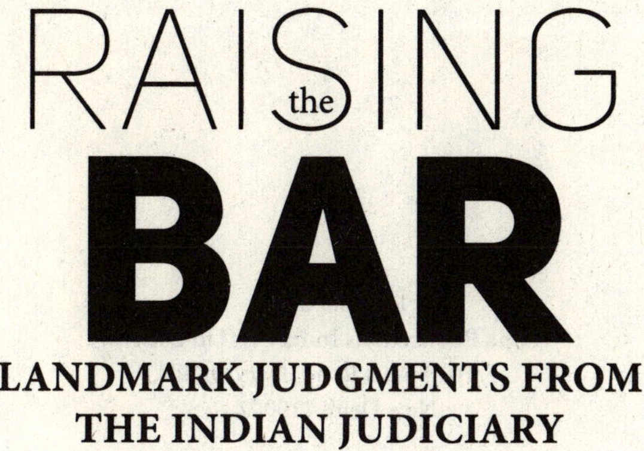

RAISING the BAR

LANDMARK JUDGMENTS FROM THE INDIAN JUDICIARY

PINKY ANAND

with **SAUDAMINI SHARMA**

RUPA

Published by
Rupa Publications India Pvt. Ltd 2024
7/16, Ansari Road, Daryaganj
New Delhi 110002

Sales centres:
Bengaluru Chennai Hyderabad
Jaipur Kathmandu Kolkata
Mumbai Prayagraj

The views and opinions expressed in this book are the author's own and the facts are as reported by her which have been verified to the extent possible, and the publishers are not in any way liable for the same.

P-ISBN: 978-93-5702-040-4
E-ISBN: 978-93-5702-056-5

First impression 2024

10 9 8 7 6 5 4 3 2 1

Printed in India

Contents

Foreword

At the outset, I congratulate Pinky Anand and Saudamini Sharma for astutely penning down the splendid compilation of landmark judgments from the Indian Judiciary under an appropriate title, *Raising the Bar*.

I have known Pinky Anand and her affection for moral use of law for many years. She has been at the helm of many famous cases, and with her experience of many decades, she has made a profoundly remarkable contribution through this book. Right from Indira Gandhi's election case to the LGBTQIA+ community rights issues, from honour killings and passive euthanasia to Sanjay Dutt case, Pinky Anand has created a consummate anthology of some of the landmark judgments with her unique style.

Her narration is lucid, insightful and inclusive of many anecdotes used as a tool to explain the complexities of legal jargon. Pinky Anand, to my utter surprise, reflects on the pages of this book, as a master storyteller. She explains the origins of some of the cases with social, political, religious and cultural backgrounds. She fathoms into the depths of perplexing issues like individual freedom juxtaposed with norms of the society. She becomes emotional at certain points, and tracks herself back on the judicial line of thinking, which underlines the fact that this legal luminary has kept intact the traits of being human and yet maintained a professional approach.

In this seminal work, Pinky Anand beckons us to traverse

the corridors of the judiciary, where the gavel of justice has reverberated through time, rendering judgments that have not only defined the law but also left an indelible mark on the socio-legal fabric of the nation. The title, *Raising the Bar*, serves as both a proclamation and a challenge, encapsulating the essence of the book.

The author sets out to elevate the discourse surrounding key judicial pronouncements, raising the intellectual bar for legal enthusiasts, practitioners and the discerning citizenry. The book serves as a testament to the dynamic nature of the Indian legal system, where landmark judgments act as milestones, charting the evolution of legal thought and practice. With her profound understanding of the intricacies of the legal landscape, the author acts as a sagacious guide, navigating readers through the labyrinth of landmark judgments. Her narrative prowess intertwines with her insightful analysis, transforming each case into a riveting legal saga with subtle human elements. As readers embark on this intellectual odyssey, they meet the mosaic of cases that have left a lasting imprint on the legal and societal canvas of India. Congratulations once again, and I wish Pinky Anand a great success in all her endeavours!

Nitin Gadkari

Minister of Road Transport & Highways

Introduction

There can be many reasons for putting pen to paper. One of the reasons for lawyers such as myself, who have accidentally accumulated around four decades of practice, are the impressions that some cases leave. It is not really the facts, or even the law, but to me, sometimes, it is the taste that they leave on my tongue. Some bitter like Aanchal; some sour like the 'ISIS brides' cases pending before the Government of India; some delightfully tangy like the case of the Murderess in Calcutta (now Kolkata). As I grow, I want to put these tastes and these emotions I have felt, when I have read a case or have been involved in one, to paper. This book is my attempt at doing so.

I am often asked why I became a lawyer. I think, besides the often repeated answer that I give—I wanted to be the change in society—it was also the thrill that I pursued. Law is an appealingly varied subject, never dealing with the same thing, and I have been fortunate enough to be involved with so many cases that have impacted the way we see the world today. It is my sincerest hope that you feel the same gamut of emotions that I did when I was writing this.

One of the most soul-wringing stories I have heard is that of a relatively unknown case in 2009. It was the story of a woman who fell in love with a man from a different caste in the then war-torn state of Kashmir. Unfortunately, in my line of work, death is a common collateral damage to the lines drawn by religion, caste and other such barriers. Another such meeting was with

Abhiram Biswal in 1985. I heard the same story and felt the same destruction, when I read about Manoj and Babli. I am appalled at the fact that this is happening even today, in times when women have scaled the highest peak in the world, and are gloriously achieving many other successful feats.

On the other hand we have cases like Bhanwari Devi—the sexual subjugation of women and the need to enforce submission in a woman from a lower class by sexual violence. This case gave birth to the Vishakha Guidelines, and subsequently, to legislation on Sexual Harassment of Women at Workplace in 2013.

While I talk about women, I believe it is important to talk about the 'ISIS brides'. It is the story of four women from Kerala who had left the country and travelled to Afghanistan to marry ISIS fighters. These women, post the deaths of their husbands in war, had been jailed in Afghanistan, and the Government of India has, since then, struck down multiple requests for their extradition citing a threat to national security. With the current change in the political situation in Afghanistan after the Taliban takeover, I believe that such national security concerns have only increased. The Supreme Court also has its hands tied since it cannot take decisions on requests for extradition involving a threat to the security of the nation. I believe that India is not the only country exercising restraint in such matters. France and Britain, too, have denied extradition requests of women from their nation, who had left to marry ISIS fighters.

Other cases are the ones circling around the privacy and autonomy of individuals. The constitutional validity of the Aadhaar Act was challenged on the grounds that it violated the individual privacy of the people holding Aadhaar card by revealing their identity and biometric information—in essence, arguably creating a state of surveillance. However, the Supreme Court, in 2018, upheld the constitutional validity of Aadhaar to the extent that it allowed authentication of individual identity by the Government for the purposes of administering social welfare benefits and schemes. I believe that the Supreme Court had rightly observed that the real issue involved was not regarding infringement of the right to individual privacy but about creating a reasonable exception to it—prioritizing public good over private good. Similarly, another landmark ruling was the one legalizing passive euthanasia and recognizing the Right to Die with Dignity as a fundamental right. It was in 2013, when the Supreme Court had first faced the question of allowing passive euthanasia for Aruna Shanbaug. However, the final verdict and guidelines legalizing euthanasia came only in 2018, and the court framed guidelines for permitting passive euthanasia.

This book, thus, delves into the intricacies of the deep-rooted religious, cultural and geopolitical issues of the Indian society, and how the judicial decisions on such matters have influenced our thinking in the present times. These are the provocative incidents that have left an indelible mark on my experience and practice over the past decades, and I hope you feel the same level of stimulation while perusing the same.

The Shadowed Legacy

Raj Narain v. Indira Gandhi, 1971

'Where the mind is without fear and the head is held high, where knowledge is free. Where the world has not been broken up into fragments by narrow domestic walls. Where words come out from the depth of truth, where tireless striving stretches its arms toward perfection. Where the clear stream of reason has not lost its way into the dreary desert sand of dead habit. Where the mind is led forward by thee into ever widening thought and action. In to that heaven of freedom, my father, LET MY COUNTRY AWAKE!'

—Rabindranath Tagore, *Gitanjali*

The year 1971 is significant in our nation's history. It was the year that we fought and ultimately won the Indo-Pak War, and were instrumental in the creation of another nation that shares its borders with us—Bangladesh.

It was also the year of a landslide victory for the Congress, which won the fifth Lok Sabha election under the leadership of Indira Gandhi, who has continued to inspire generations of young women as the ultimate symbol of women in power. The 1971 victory was a thumping one for the Congress. Overcoming a split in the party, the Congress regained all the seats it had lost previously.

The stupendous win, however, was also not an ethical one. Mrs Gandhi had called for the fifth general election, a year ahead of schedule, in March 1971. Many conjectured that the entire thing had been manipulated. The theme and slogan of Indira Gandhi's election campaign was *Garibi Hatao Desh Bachao* (Remove poverty, save the country), which has, till date, not lost relevance as a spectacle in power play. However, it was during this time that the Congress split ideologically and words like electoral malpractice gained traction. Fresh off the back of a huge war victory, Mrs Gandhi created a foolproof campaign, the end result of which was leading her party to a two-thirds majority in the Lok Sabha, successfully consolidating power.

CHALLENGING PM ELECTION

However, the celebrations were short lived. Raj Narain, a well-known freedom fighter and leader of Ram Manohar Lohia's Samyukta Socialist Party (SSP), who had contested against Mrs Gandhi from the Raebareli constituency in Uttar Pradesh, filed a petition in the Allahabad High Court on 24 April 1971 challenging the Prime Minister's (PM) election, alleging electoral irregularities.

In the time between the filing of the petition and the passing of the verdict, the tide had begun to change for Mrs Gandhi and her government. In 1973, the economy, the polity and the credibility of Mrs Gandhi's leadership and her government had taken a hit. Even though Mrs Gandhi's 1971 election campaign had revolved around the slogan of 'Garibi Hatao', people's expectations remained unfulfilled after she was elected. No more than little dents were being made towards alleviating rural and urban poverty and economic inequality, and caste and class oppression had continued to be rampant. The government's capacity to redress the situation had been seriously impaired by growing corruption in most areas of governance and the widespread belief that the higher-ups of the ruling party were involved in it.

On 12 June 1975, Justice Jagmohanlal Sinha of the Allahabad High Court gave his judgment finding Indira Gandhi guilty of electoral malpractices. It invalidated Mrs Gandhi's election and disbarred her from office for six years. She was held guilty of corrupt practices committed under Section 123(7) of the Representation of the People Act, by having obtained the assistance of Yashpal Kapur, a gazetted officer in the Government of India, in furtherance of her election prospects. The judgment has forever been etched in the history of Indian politics as it was the first time ever that a PM's election was invalidated.

This momentous victory was overshadowed by the 20-day stay order by Justice Sinha, giving time sought by Mrs Gandhi's counsel, so that an appeal could be filed in the Supreme Court of India before the order could take effect. In the years to come, this decision would prove to be one of those crucial moments that were detrimental to the emergence of what was known as the darkest period of Indian democracy. This was the first of many fatal victories that were to follow.

Amidst the criticism and protests from the opposition party, the appeal in the Supreme Court was filed and on 24 June 1975, the vacation judge bench of the Supreme Court presided by Justice V.R. Krishna Iyer, granted a conditional stay of the High Court judgment. It allowed Mrs Gandhi to be a Member of Parliament but barred her from presiding over parliamentary proceedings, which meant that she could address Parliament but couldn't participate and vote in the Lok Sabha debates and could not draw remuneration as a member. Even though the stay imposed conditions seemingly restricting the powers of the PM, it was the next day that the nation would witness how truly powerful and astounding her capabilities still were.

In 1974, the Opposition had started to gain momentum, and was materializing in the form of the JP movement, accusing Mrs Gandhi's government of major corruption. After the verdict was stayed, the Opposition began staging protest rallies against Indira Gandhi's rule across the country. It was at this time of political calamity that Mrs Gandhi turned to her son Sanjay Gandhi for support and advice, who ultimately convinced her to keep fighting the battle inside as well as outside the courtroom.

Under Jayaprakash Narayan's leadership, who was often called the 'Lok Nayak', the Opposition led a massive political rally in Delhi's Ramlila Maidan on 25 June, where he announced a nationwide Satyagraha demanding Mrs Gandhi's resignation, and requested the army, police and government employees not to obey 'illegal and immoral orders'. The government perceived this as an incitement and feared that it would bring all government machinery to a halt. Meanwhile, railway employees, too, gave a call for a nationwide strike led by George Fernandes.

Sensing the moment to be ripe, the PM played her ultimate card. On the night of 25 June 1975, Indira Gandhi, accompanied by her trusted advisor Siddhartha Shankar Ray, then the chief minister of West Bengal, went to meet President Fakhruddin Ali Ahmed to sign off on the one plan of action that would guarantee her reign.

It was just before midnight when, with one stroke of the President's pen, fate of India changed forever. Emergency was declared throughout the nation. Fundamental rights of the citizens were suspended. The PM had the authority to rule by decree and had the power to suspend elections and civil liberties. Indira Gandhi effectively became a dictator.

The reasons cited for imposing Emergency were internal disturbances and a grave crisis plaguing the nation—a necessity likely born out of desperation and ambition. The nation was stunned with anger. Democracy had been hijacked to serve personal interests. It was the ultimate betrayal and the implications were extraordinarily staggering.

Top leaders of the Opposition, namely Jayprakash Narayan, Morarji Desai, Atal Bihari Vajpayee, L.K. Advani, Arun Jaitley, Vijaya Raje Scindia, Siddaramaiah and M.K. Stalin, were detained and arrested without any reason in the dead of night. Electricity was cut off from Bahadur Shah Zafar Marg, the Fleet Street of India, where the offices of almost all the national dailies were located. The press was censored, and electricity was restored only after the censorship apparatus had been set up. All newspapers needed to get prior approval for any material that was to be published. Apprehending social and communal disharmony, the Rashtriya Swayamsevak Sangh (RSS) and Jamaat-e-Islami were banned. Protests, strikes and public agitations were also disallowed.

The reign of terror was unending. People were arrested and detained simply on the assumption that they might commit an offence. The Shah Commission later estimated that nearly 1,11,000 people were arrested under preventive detention laws—higher than the number of arrests made during the 1942 Quit India Movement. Custodial deaths were common occurrence during the Emergency. The federal distribution of powers was suspended, with power concentrated in the hands of the Union Government. Chaos was rampant as power was placed in the hands of an extra-constitutional authority. Citing welfare, forced sterilization drives in Delhi were carried out, spearheaded by Sanjay Gandhi.

In the name of beautification and cleansing the state, demolition drives took place at Turkman Gate, where the protesting slum residents were subjected to police brutality and were run over by bulldozers.

The fears of one individual had jeopardized the very fate of Indian democracy. It was as if the country and its people were transported back in time when we were all slaves and any hint of revolt meant unprecedented State-sponsored retaliation. The ethos of the largest democracy in the world changed overnight, dictated by an autocratic power.

The only uncertain variable that remained was the case pending against Mrs Gandhi in the Supreme Court. In order to assure her victory, she had approached one of the most brilliant legal minds of the time—Nani Palkhivala, who had argued and won the stay order. However, after the declaration of the Emergency, Palkhivala did what no one had anticipated. He valiantly returned the brief he had accepted to defend the PM. To do so at the pinnacle of the PM's power was nothing short of heroic, for it could have meant dire consequences for him. In doing so, he not only refused to represent Indira Gandhi in court but also demonstrated that he was completely against the step taken by her in declaring the Emergency.

On 7 November 1975, the Supreme Court of the country was ready to deliver its verdict against the 'unseating' judgment of the High Court. In order to understand the outcome of the verdict, it is imperative to know and understand the rationale behind it. The Constitution bench delivering the historic judgment had three main issues under its consideration: the constitutional validity of Clause (4) Article 329A inserted vide The Constitution (Thirty-Ninth Amendment) Act; whether Representation of the People (Amendment) Act, 1974, and the Election Laws (Amendment) Act, 1975, were constitutionally valid; and whether the election of Indira Gandhi was void. The issues all revolved around The Constitution (Thirty-Ninth Amendment) Act.

In the months preceding the judgment, and after the

pronouncement of the High Court verdict, the ruling government had pushed for and succeeded in amending major changes in the election laws as well as in the Constitution itself. Two months after the 'unseating' verdict, on 10 August 1975, The Constitution (Thirty-Ninth Amendment) Act was passed. It inserted two new Articles in the Constitution (Articles 71 and 329A) while adding three acts in the Ninth Schedule: the Representation of the People Act, 43, of 1951, the Representation of the People (Amendment) Act, 58, of 1974, and the Election Laws (Amendment) Act, 40, of 1975. All these amendments were a means to an end—one that would eventually serve to validate the annulled election of the PM by the High Court. The court had declared that Mrs Gandhi had to be regarded as a candidate from 29 December 1970 as she held herself out on that date as a candidate. The date of the announcement of her candidacy was crucial to determine other allegations against her.

The second matter was that of Yashpal Kapur's role in Mrs Gandhi's election. Even though it was sought to be proved by the Party that Kapur had not acted in his capacity as a gazetted officer within the Government of India as he had already tendered his resignation before Mrs Gandhi had sought him out, it was eventually proved that his resignation had not become effective after he had already rendered his assistance to Mrs Gandhi.

Justice Sinha's verdict further held that Mrs Gandhi and her election agent Yashpal Kapur had procured and obtained the assistance of the officers of the state government, particularly the district magistrate, the superintendent of police, the executive engineer of the Public Works Department (PWD) and the engineer to Hydel Department for the construction of rostrums and arrangement of supply of power for loudspeakers at campaign meetings addressed by Mrs Gandhi on 1 February 1971 and 25 February 1971.

Even though it had been less than five months since the controversial High Court judgment had been pronounced, drastic changes had taken place in election and constitutional law by the time the appeal was finally heard by the Supreme Court Constitution Bench.

In the case of the constitutional validity of Clause (4) of Article 329A, it was argued by the contesting party that it destroyed the basic structure of the Constitution, and that the constitution of the House which passed the Constitution (Thirty-ninth Amendment) Act was illegal.

Clause (4) of Article 329A stated:

(i) No law made by Parliament before the commencement of the Constitution (Thirty-Ninth Amendment) Act, 1975, in so far as it relates to the election petitions and matters connected therewith shall apply or shall be deemed even to have applied to or in relation to the election of any such person as is referred to in Clause (1) to either House of Parliament;

(ii) and such election shall not be deemed to be void or ever to have become void on any ground on which such election could be declared to be void or has before such commencement been declared to be void under any such law;

(iii) and notwithstanding any order made by any court before such commencement declaring such election to be void, such election shall continue to be valid in all respects;

(iv) and any such order and any finding on which such order is based shall be and shall be deemed always to have been void and of no effect.

The above clause was, in effect, to bar the jurisdiction of the Supreme Court from entertaining the matter. This amendment made the election of the president, PM, Vice President and Speaker of Lok Sabha above scrutiny and unjustifiable in courts of law.

The Five-Judge bench applied the basic structure laid down in the landmark judgment of *Kesavananda Bharati v. State of Kerala, 1973*. It was held that Clause (4) of Article 329A is liable to be struck down on the grounds that it violates the principle of free and fair elections, which is an important part of the Constitution. It abolishes the forum without providing for another forum for going into the dispute relating to the validity of the election of the accused candidate, and further prescribes that the said dispute shall not be governed by any election law and that the validity of said election shall be absolute and not consequently be liable to be assailed, and it extinguishes both the right and the remedy to challenge the validity of the aforesaid election. As per Article 329(b), election disputes are to be presented to such an authority as the legislature may by law provide. The nature of the dispute raised in an election petition is such that it can only be resolved by a judicial process. It held that Clause (4) of Article 329A takes away these rights and should therefore be struck down. Justice Khanna while delivering the judgment observed:

> To confer an absolute validity upon the election of one particular candidate and to prescribe that the validity of that election shall not be questioned before any forum or under any law would necessarily have the effect of saying that howsoever gross may be the improprieties which might have vitiated that election, howsoever flagrant may be the malpractices which might have been committed on behalf of the returned candidate during the course of the election and howsoever foul and violative of the principles of free and fair elections may be the means which might have been employed for securing success in that election, the said election would be none-the-less valid and it would

> not be permissible to complain of those improprieties, malpractices and unfair means before any forum or under any law with a view to assail the validity of that election. Not much argument is needed to show that any provision which brings about that result is subversive of the principle of free and fair election in a democracy. The fact that the candidate concerned is the Prime Minister of the country or the Speaker of the lower House of Parliament would, if anything, add force to the above conclusion because both these offices represent the acme of the democratic process in a country.

With regards to the contention that the constitution of the House which passed The Constitution (Thirty-Ninth Amendment) Act was illegal, the court held that the issue essentially relates to the validity of the proceedings of the two Houses of Parliament. Such matters were not justiciable and pertained to the internal domain of the two Houses. It observed that the Court could not go into the question of whether the sittings of the Houses of Parliament are not constitutionally valid because some members of those Houses have been prevented from attending and participating in the discussions in those Houses.

It was argued by Raj Narain that a number of members of the two Houses of Parliament were being illegally detained by executive orders before the summoning of the two Houses and that was made possible by the President making an order under Article 359 of the Constitution on 27 June 1975, which precluded these members from moving the court and obtaining release from illegal detention and attending the session.

The court said that the President, in performing his constitutional function under Articles 352 and 359, had not authorized the illegal detention of any person, let alone any

Member of Parliament or unconstitutionally prevented the release from custody of any member. He had only discharged his constitutional functions.

Justice Beg relied on Article 122 of the Constitution which prevents the Supreme Court from going into any question relating to irregularities of proceeding in the Parliament while rejecting the above contention. The then Chief Justice of India, Justice A.N. Ray held that, 'When a member is excluded from participating in the proceedings of the House, that is a matter concerning Parliament and the grievance of exclusion is in regard to proceedings within the walls of Parliament. In regard to rights to be exercised within the walls of the House, the House itself is the judge.'

On the issue of the constitutional validity of Representation of the People (Amendment) Act, 1974, and the Election Laws (Amendment) Act, 1975, the argument presented by the Mr Narain's counsel was that these Acts destroy or damage the basic structure or basic features of the Constitution.

While deciding on the issue of the three Acts inserted in the Ninth Schedule, the Chief Justice held:

> The constitutional validity of a statute depends entirely on the existence of the legislative power and the express provision in Article 13. Apart from the limitation, the legislature is not subject to any other prohibition. The amendments made to the 1951 Act by the Amendment Acts, 1974 and 1975, are to give effect to certain views expressed by this court in preference to certain views departed from or otherwise to clarify the original intention. It is within the powers of Parliament to frame laws with regard to elections. Parliament has power to enumerate and define election expenses. Parliament has power to lay down limits

> on election expenses. Parliament has power to state whether certain expenses can be included or may be excluded from election expenses. Parliament has power to adopt conclusive proof with regard to matters of appointment, resignation or termination of service. Parliament has power to state what can be considered to be office of profit. Parliament has power to state as to what will and what will not constitute corrupt practice. Parliament has power to enact what will be the ground for disqualification. Parliament has power to define 'candidate'. Parliament has power to state what symbols will be allotted to candidates at election. These are all legislative policies.

The bench held that giving retrospective effect to legislative amendment is accepted to be a valid exercise of legislative power. Retrospective operation of any law would cause hardship to some persons or other. This is inevitable; but that is no reason to deny to the legislature the power to enact retrospective law. In the case of a law that has retrospective effect, the theory is that the law was actually in operation in the past and if the provision of the Acts are general in their operation, there can be no challenge to them on the ground of discrimination or unfairness merely because of their retrospective effect.

Justice Khanna, while holding Act 40 of 1975 valid and not suffering from any constitutional infirmity held, that in view of the finding that the provisions of the Act under consideration had not been shown to impinge upon the process of free and fair elections and thereby to strike at the basic structure of the Constitution, it was not necessary to deal with the argument that the validity of Act 40 of 1975 cannot be assailed on the ground that it strikes at the basic structure. The argument of invalidity of the above-mentioned acts were thus rejected unanimously, meaning that the law was valid.

Deliberation on the charges of commission of corrupt practice and whether the election of Mrs Gandhi was void was met with serious resistance, particularly since there were categorical findings of the High Court holding her liable. However, while deciding on the said issues, the Supreme Court had to operate on an entirely different footing, as the electoral laws had been changed retrospectively to facilitate the PM's innocence. All the grounds on which the election of the PM was held to be void were no longer tenable as they had been categorically amended one after the other post the High Court judgment.

The definition of the word 'candidate' was changed under Section 123(7) of The People's Representative (Amendment) Act to establish that Mrs Gandhi had filed her nomination on 1 February 1975 and hence a candidate post that date. Therefore any help that she took from government officers before that date could not be considered a corrupt practice, thus nullifying the finding of the High Court that the appellant had obtained and procured the assistance of Yashpal Kapur during the period 7 January 1971 to 24 January 1971.

The High Court, finding that Yashpal Kapur had continued to be in the service of the Government of India till 25 January1971, which was the date of the notification regarding the acceptance of Yashpal Kapur's resignation, was resolved in the following manner. The said notification held that the President was pleased 'to accept the resignation of Shri Y.P.R. Kapoor, Officer on Special Duty in the Prime Minister's Secretariat, with effect from the fore noon of the 14 January, 1971'. In view of the newly added explanation to Section 123 of the Representation of the People Act, it had to be held that his resignation had come into effect from 14 January 1971. The defeated candidate's counsel alleged that Kapur had made several speeches during 7 January 1971 to 25 January 1971, supporting Indira Gandhi's candidature, but the court found no evidence to support that he made those speeches with the approval of or on the request of Mrs Gandhi.

Justice Khanna had held that Mrs Gandhi:

> […]can still be not guilty of the commission of corrupt practice under Section 123(7) of the RP Act in view of the new proviso which has been inserted at the end of Clause (7) of Section 123 and which reads as under:
>
> Provided that where any person, in the service of the Government and belonging to any of the classes aforesaid, in the discharge or purported discharge of his official duty, makes any arrangements or provides any facilities or does any other act or thing, for, to or in relation to any candidate or his agent or any other person acting with the consent of the candidate or his election agent, (whether by reason of the office held by the candidate or for any other reason), such arrangements, facilities or act or thing shall not be deemed to be assistance for the furtherance of the prospects of that candidate's election.' The above proviso has also a direct bearing on the allegation of the respondent that the appellant committed corrupt practice under Section 123(7) of the RP Act inasmuch as she or her election agent procured the assistance of members of armed forces of the Union for furtherance of her election prospects because of the fact that the members of the armed forces arranged planes and helicopters of the Air Force for her flights to enable her to address meetings in her constituency.

The argument that the election of Indira Gandhi was void on the grounds that she had exceeded the limit of authorized expenditure during election campaigning of ₹35,000 was rejected by the court. It was held as per sections 83(1)(b) and 123(6) of The People's Representative Act, 1951, that 'voluntary expenditure by friends, relations or sympathizers and expenditure incurred by a candidate's party without any request or authorization by the candidate has never been deemed to be expenditure by the candidate herself.' The court further stated that as per Section 77 of The People's Representative Act, 1951, 'expenditure incurred by a political party in connection with the election of the candidates of the party is not a part of the election expenses of the candidate. Similarly participation in the programme of activity organized by a political party will not fall within the election expenses of the candidate of the party.'

The Supreme Court verdict delivered on 7 November 1975 declared that Clauses (4) and (5) of Article 329A was unconstitutional as being violative of the basic structure of the Constitution of India. It held the Representation of People's (Amendment) Act, 1974, and Election Laws (Amendment) Act, 1975, were considered to be legal, constitutionally valid and free from all infirmities. The election of Indira Gandhi, from her constituency Raebareli, was considered to be valid. The Judgment set aside the Allahabad High Court verdict of 12 June 1975, and removed all corruption charges levied against Mrs Gandhi, acquitting her.

The entireties of the events were a rarity in itself. It was the first time that a constitutional amendment was struck down on the basic structural doctrine that had been propounded a couple of years ago in the Kesavananda Bharati case. It was the first time people witnessed the PM of the country come to court and testify. It was also the first time that election laws were retrospectively amended to validate the annulled election of a PM.

While the Judiciary had successfully protected the Constitution, in the end, the amended laws that were so blatantly self-serving accomplished their sole purpose. The PM was fully empowered to run the country as she saw fit.

The Emergency lasted for 21 months. It was only on 18 January 1977 that the PM surprised the nation with an unscheduled broadcast announcing fresh elections and the release of all political prisoners. So, 21 March 1977 marked the official end to the 21-month long draconian Emergency. Unbeknownst to the public hatred of the Emergency, Mrs Gandhi had miscalculated her victory in the forthcoming elections and underestimated the Opposition's strategy.

Two months later, in a stunning election outcome, Indira Gandhi and her party were swept from office. Both Sanjay Gandhi and his mother were defeated in their respective Lok Sabha seats of Raebareli and Amethi. For the first time since Independence, the Congress was defeated in the Lok Sabha elections. For the first time since Independence, a party other than the Congress was going to govern at the Centre. On 24 March 1977, Morarji Desai became the PM of India.

Succeeding Mrs Gandhi, Desai led the Janata Party government till 1980. That government, however, collapsed within two years due to infighting amongst the leaders of the various parties. This then led to the split of the Janata Party and eventually the formation of the Bharatiya Janata Party (BJP). In the 1980 Lok Sabha polls, Mrs Gandhi returned to power and remained in power till her assassination in 1984.

The case of *Indira Nehru Gandhi v. Raj Narain (1976) 2 SCR 347*, needs to be remembered for the lasting impact it had on our history, politics and law. Not only did it trigger an Emergency but also revealed how vulnerable our judiciary, legislature and press are to a person with power and ambition.

Let us never forget that democracy was taken away from us for 21 months, when time had stood still. Let us not forget the regressive regime that our nation had to endure for those 21 months, let us never let that happen again.

Indian unity has shown the strength to withstand wars, rebellions, crises and disasters, but it is only as strong as its democracy, for it is democracy that gives every Indian a stake in their country's present and future.

In the words of the architect of our constitution, Dr B.R. Ambedkar, 'Political democracy cannot last unless there lies at the base of it social democracy. What does social democracy mean? It means a way of life which recognizes liberty, equality and fraternity as the principles of life.'

In the Name of Honour

Cases of Honour Killing

Sometime in September 2009, I met Anchal Sharma. She was of a slight built with jet black hair. But it was her eyes that struck me the most. They were the eyes of a woman who had seen horrors one could only imagine and was desperate for answers and succour. This wasn't the first time I had seen a distressed woman. And, unfortunately, it wasn't the last time either. In my line of work, they are all too common: domestic violence, abandonment, family or marital troubles and, rarely, women looking for their share of the property.

Anchal was different, and so was her story. She contacted me and narrated her ordeal over endless cups of coffee and quite a few breakdowns. Her story was not just her story, but the story of so many countless women irrespective of class or caste or religion.

Anchal's former name was Amina Yousef, and she belonged to a family that owned houseboats in Srinagar. She met Rajneesh Sharma, a businessman from Jammu, who owned an aluminium fabrication workshop. He had come to Kashmir for the Amarnath Yatra and had spent a few days in a houseboat that Anchal's family owned. He asked for her number before leaving for the yatra. They soon started speaking regularly once he was back in Srinagar. In a moment reminiscent of a Bollywood movie, her face lit up as she recounted those details of her life. Their affair continued for seven years.

In a state scarred with religious fault lines, this was not the wisest choice. But love knows no language or religion. During the 2008 Amarnath agitation, they would speak over the phone continuously, barely being able to afford the huge telephone bills, but always talking to each other amidst the clarion calls of the religious warriors. The sound of war was often the background score of their conversations, and it seemed like fate was trying to warn them.

The story went on as all stories do. After seven years of being apart, the two finally decided to get married. In August, Anchal told her mother that she was leaving to meet Rajneesh and left for the airport, where Rajneesh was waiting for her. They took the flight to Jammu where they got married, and the Kashmiri Amina became Jammu's Anchal Sharma. Little did they know what destiny had in store for them. After getting married, the two went for their honeymoon and returned to Jammu in September 2009.

On a crisp autumn night in September, the couple had settled in at Rajneesh's brother's house when the police arrived, accompanied by Anchal's brothers. That was the very night when Anchal's world was torn apart. Her brothers were shouting curses and they caught Rajneesh's sister-in-law by her hair. When she asked the police to intervene, one of Anchal's brothers yelled that they had paid off the police both in Kashmir and Jammu. On hearing the commotion, the newly-weds tried to escape through a backdoor. In all the panic, they found themselves separated. Anchal remembers Rajneesh's brother Pawan shouting her name. It was then that Rajneesh came back to the house, fearing that Anchal had fallen off the stairs in her hurry to join him. There, the police pounced on him, bundled him into their vehicle and drove off.

Rajneesh was produced in court two days later, but with the name of Pawan Sharma. He was injured, Anchal told me, but no medical check-up had been done and no reports had been produced. It was apparent that he had been tortured. On 5 October, he was again produced before a magistrate and that was the last day he was seen alive. They later told Anchal that Rajneesh had committed suicide in his cell. But she knew that he had been murdered by the police because he had dared to marry a Muslim from Srinagar.

The records I received from her said that Rajneesh's first postmortem had been done at Srinagar but was inconsequential, while the second one done at Jammu reported telltale signs of police torture. We filed a petition in the Supreme Court asking for a CBI enquiry, which was granted in 2013, almost three years after the petition had been filed. I am told that after some time, Anchal went back to her parents and changed her statement to say that she had been abducted by Rajneesh and forcibly converted and married.

Since then, I have often been asked if this end was not an insult to her crusade. I don't think so. Life has to go on, and we all make compromises to enable us to survive, especially one who has been witness to such senseless death of a beloved. One thing is clear—Anchal Sharma is a brave woman.

Another case, very early in my career, happened in Delhi. When I started my career in 1985, there were certain cases that somehow decided the way my life would be. One of these cases was of Abhiram Biswal. When I met Abhiram, he was a teacher and married to a woman called Farah Mohammed. Farah was a student in Delhi's Jawaharlal Nehru University. When Farah went missing from Delhi, it was nearly two months later, that Abhiram discovered her whereabouts. She had been taken to Karachi. How she had reached there, or what had happened there is anybody's guess. She wrote to her husband, asking to be rescued, or be given poison to die. She had been imprisoned at her aunt's place. As all such stories go, she was said to have sustained burns in October

1989 and finally passed away in January 1990, just a few months after her impassioned appeal for help and rescue.

The politics between India and Pakistan have been strained at best and war-like at worst. The year 1989 was a time when the diplomacy between our countries was not at its strongest. However, Abhiram wanted to see his wife one last time. A criminal case of kidnapping against her father and other relatives could only be filed after bringing extraordinary political pressure on the police. The petition for Habeas Corpus could not succeed, simply because she had allegedly gone of her own volition and had left the jurisdiction of the Indian courts. Despite being an Indian national, and her father and mother being highly educated, this was a woman who was forcibly taken to Pakistan by her own parents and killed for the sin of falling in love with a boy from another religion. In a country where 'diversity' is the first word we learn in schools while describing our magnificent nation, this was against our very foundations.

I am often stunned by the dichotomies that our society functions in. It has bothered me that the kind of problems and issues I have come across for most of my career would not have arisen had we simply agreed and stayed on the path we were taught as children.

In Indian society, honour is often considered an almost inalienable part of life. For us, it holds so much importance that any discredit or defamation to honour is regarded as a physical affront and can be penalized under criminal laws. The regard for this concept of 'honour' or '*izzat*', and the paramountcy given to it becomes the cause for some serious contentious situations and events in India. The idea that love for izzat sometimes overtakes filial love is not just terrifying, but points to an extremely dysfunctional interpretation of what constitutes a healthy society.

We are taught that love trumps all, and I have often wondered how our elders and the society forgets the asterisk attached to it: if you fall in love with a person from the opposite sex, love trumps all; if you fall in love with a person of the same economic background, love trumps all; if the other person is not a divorcee and has had a relatively non-controversial past, love trumps all; if the other person is acceptable by societal standards, only then does love trump all.

Another one that we often hear is: 'Your family loves you and will stand by you'. Unfortunately, for many of us, this *shiksha* has not stood the test of time. Your family loves you and will stand by you for anything unless you choose a partner who's not to their liking.

We are social beings, and it is often repeated that family is the basic unit that shapes our personality. And in the middle of this extremely sacred thread of how important family is, we often forget to see the cruelties meted out by family members to those who dare to marry or love outside the boundaries created by the very same family.

As human beings, one of the foundational rights conferred upon us is the right to choose a partner with whom we can spend our lives. As a society, we live within a certain set of rules and parameters, and often these parameters, instead of leading us towards a righteous life, become oppressive and impinge on our basic liberties.

When I regard the society we live in, I often feel that the concept of 'familial honour' takes precedence over our personal choices. We try to associate our actions to familial prestige and status. We put our kids in the best schools, often not for the education but because we are trying to keep up with the Joneses. Some of us force our beliefs upon our children and deny them partners of their choosing because they are not of the right caste or *gotra*. The worst manifestation of this is what we know as 'honour killing'.

Honour killing is not a foreign concept. I suspect, it roots from the invasions of our lands where parents, in an attempt to protect their children from forced marriages to the invaders, used to kill their own children. It is an extremely debased and corrupt practice, wherein guardians of family honour tend to kill their child to prevent them from marrying a person not of their choice. Prestige-based crimes are usually seen in a patriarchal society, where family status is a priority.

In sociological terms, such violence is understood to be derived from a desire to control the behaviour of women within a community, most often with an emphasis on her sexuality. There are many choices that come under scrutiny of these self-styled keepers of honour, including clothing, communication with men and sexual relationships. Victims of familial violence are targeted because their behaviour is seen to violate cultural or religious norms, where their assailant feels that the only way to prevent such behaviour or restore family respect is to harm or kill the victim. Ultimately, such an interpretation of honour is grounded in an objectification of women and the idea that the honour of a family is vested in her choice of a partner.

The worst aspect of these crimes is that they often have a collective dimension and are usually planned by several family members. Whilst there are a number of forms of such crimes, including bodily mutilation and acid attacks, amongst the most severe manifestations is honour killing. Victims are buried alive, burnt, shot, smothered, stabbed, stoned and strangled to death. The lack of empathy and freedom of choice has led to women being murdered for a variety of trivial reasons, including talking to an unrelated man, using X (formerly known as Twitter) or Facebook, refusing an arranged marriage, seeking a divorce or disobeying her husband or father.

There is a marked difference between an 'honour killing' and a 'crime of passion'. The former conveys the intention of the perpetrator, and in doing so, invariably implies a rationale behind the act. The main point of distinction between the two is the degree of forethought, since crimes of passion are unplanned and impulsive while honour killings require pre-meditated thought, and, unfortunately, often involves the participation of society. These are proof of a range of violent and non-violent manifestations of women's commodification in patriarchal societies. Another dismal variant of honour killing is honour suicide, where members of the family force the perceived transgressor to take their life.

The crime of honour killing is recognized under international law as violence against women, since it violates the Right to Life. International law requires States to prevent gender-based violence. As per international law, 'honour' is not a substantial or a legally valid defence for such acts.

It also flouts the Convention on the Elimination of All Forms of Discrimination Against Women, 1979 (CEDAW). As per Article 1 of the Convention, the term 'discrimination against women' means any distinction, exclusion or restriction made on the basis of sex which has the effect or purpose of impairing or nullifying the recognition, enjoyment or exercise by women, irrespective of their marital status, on a basis of equality of men and women, of human rights and fundamental freedoms in the political, economic, social, cultural, civil or any other field.

India is one of the signatories to this UN Charter among 185 other countries worldwide. Honour killing violates both the letter and spirit of this law. An honour killing is cold blooded and planned murder executed to somehow try and retrieve a misbegotten sense of honour. We need to understand that the death of a spouse is a watershed moment in a partner's life. It changes them, psychologically and emotionally, and puts them on a new path. For some, it acts as a blow, motivating the victim's loved ones to fight for change, as was the case of Kausalya.

Kausalya was the daughter of an auto driver, belonging to the Dindigul district of Tamil Nadu. She was a bright student, scoring enough in her exams to earn admission to an engineering college. In 2014, the first day of her college, she met a boy called Sankar, who proposed to her, and over the next six months, their friendship blossomed into romance. Her parents did not approve of the relationship because Sankar was from the Dalit Pallar community. Kausalya was an upper-caste Thevar. After many fights and arguments, the young couple decided to get married, and Kausalya dropped out of college in March 2015 and moved to her husband's house.

A month after the move, Chinnsamy, Kausalya's father, tried to forcibly separate the two by abducting her. She could only be retrieved when her husband filed a missing person's report. Kausalya's father also tried to bribe Sankar with ₹10 lakh to end the marriage, but to no avail. After all these efforts had not proven fruitful, the father of the bride decided to hire killers to kill the man his daughter loved and had married.

Almost a year after the marriage, on 12 March 2016, the couple left their house to buy a new shirt for Sankar, when they were accosted by six men on bikes. The murder was committed in front of a huge crowd, slashing the couple with knives on a busy bus stop. Sankar died on the way to the hospital, having sustained 34 stab wounds.

Kausalya was strong. She testified against her entire family and ended up getting justice for her slain husband, eventually turning her experience into motivation for working against casteism and fighting for Dalit rights. She eventually remarried in 2018 to a man of her own caste. The matter is still in court.

The story is relevant because it's one of the very few that turned pain to strength to try and create a change. There are unfortunately far more stories of a ghastly nature, of a murder most gruesome in the name of honour.

MANOJ-BABLI INCIDENT

Belonging to the same village of Karora, Kaithal district in Haryana, both Manoj Banwala and Babli were the sole breadwinners of their families. They got to know each other and soon fell in love. They were warned several times by their elders that such a liaison would cause grave problems to them. They paid no heed and soon eloped. The problem was that the village elders had decided that since they both belonged to the same village, they were considered to be related and their marriage was considered to be incestuous in their eyes.

On 6 April 2007, they eloped to Chandigarh to get married. The marriage was solemnized on 7 April. However, Babli's mother filed an FIR against Manoj and his family at the Rajound Police Station on 24 April. Anticipating an arrest because of the FIR, Manoj filed an application for anticipatory bail in the Sessions Court on 12 June, and after four days, both were produced before the court of the Additional Chief Judicial Magistrate. Babli recorded a statement in which she said that she had married and eloped with Manoj of her own accord and none of Manoj's family members had been involved in it, and that she was not under threat from anybody. After recording the statement, the court directed head constable Dharampal and constable Satbir to escort the couple and drop them off safely back to Chandigarh from Rajound.

The whole situation seemed rigged from the start. The High

Court judgment records that sub-inspector Jagbir Singh had directed the constable to deboard the bus at some station. Jagbir Singh had then followed the bus and met up with the police party at village Malikpur. In another vehicle, Babli's maternal uncle, his sons, her paternal aunt's husband and their sons had been chasing them. The police constable had left the couple at Pipli bus stand after obtaining their written consent that they had desired to go ahead alone, without a police escort.

Manoj had informed his mother about all of this. He had also told her about Babli's family members following them and that they were proceeding towards Delhi. When Manoj's cousin later tried calling his mobile number, it was switched off. Manoj's family searched for the couple but they could not locate them. Later in the evening, a call was received in the Butana Police Station, stating that a girl and a boy had been forcefully pulled off from the bus and abducted by 15–16 people in a Scorpio headed towards Karnal. The information was sent to the Police Control Room as well.

Manoj's mother, after several failed attempts of contacting her son, lodged a complaint in the Butana Police Station, alleging the abduction of her son. After investigation by officials, who received reports from locals, Manoj and Babli's mutilated bodies were found at different locations. Their bodies had been carried away by the canal in which they had been dumped.

Babli's body was found with her feet and hands tied with rope. Part of the neck, and fingers of the right hand and foot were missing. Manoj's ears, eyes and lips had been mutilated. His face was not identifiable and his penis and scrotum had also been mutilated. A plastic rope was tied around the neck, and the other end was tied around both legs and knee joints with a knot.

Post mortem of the bodies revealed that Manoj had been strangulated and Babli had been administered Endosulfan. The clothes recovered from the bodies were identified by the family members as that of Manoj and Babli's. The accused were arrested soon after and their disclosure statements were recorded. The police found a lot of evidence against the accused as the victims' hair strands, hair clip and burnt pieces of photos were discovered from their car. A baton and a *ghunghru* made of silver were discovered from one of the accused's Maruti car. There were also blood stains on the right door in the rear.

The trial court at Kaithal convicted the accused under the Sections 302, 364 and 120B of the Indian Penal Code (IPC), 1860, and declared the death penalty. The trial court awarded Manoj's mother a compensation of ₹1 lakh. However, the High Court of Punjab and Haryana at Chandigarh reduced the punishment from death penalty to imprisonment for 20 years. The High Court acquitted all the accused from the charges under Section 120B (for criminal conspiracy) of the IPC, 1860:

> The family members of Babli were deprived of the love and affection of Babli for about two long months. A neighbour had taken away the girl and got her married. They had been confronted with a disturbed mental feeling. There was no criminal antecedents brought to our notice qua the accused. Nothing has been shown before this Court that the accused could not be reformed during jail sentence. Just because it is a case of hollow honour killing, we cannot jump to a conclusion that the case squarely shall not choose to incline that it is squarely falls under the category of rarest of rare cases.

A Special Leave Petition filed by the mother of the deceased is still pending in the Supreme Court. This case highlights two major issues: one, pertaining to the role of how communal mentality affects us as a society; and second relates to how honour killing, while in actuality a horrifying and barbaric planned crime, is in judicial terms a simple murder punishable under Section 302 of the IPC. As far as the first issue is concerned, in the present case, it was aggravated by the belief system of the community. The collective identity of a group in this case took precedence over their identities as human beings. It was this thought process that led the entire village to not just murder the couple but actually condone the barbaric act.

The second issue is of a legislative nature. The IPC categorizes honour killing under the category of murder. The only difference is that the intent of committing murder in the case of honour killing is clearly defined. Against this backdrop, there is an immense need to recategorize crimes related to honour because they are increasing in number. Moreover, such crimes are as heinous and grave as rape or any such demonic crime categorized as a separate offence. The law framed should be extremely strict so that there is adequate punishment for such crimes, which deters even the thought of committing such offences. If a family does not approve of the choice of their child's spouse, then the maximum they should be allowed to do is withdraw themselves from continuing any relationship with their children. Nothing in this world gives them the liberty to kill their children.

LAW AGAINST HONOUR KILLING

The problem of interference of family members to the extent of threatening the lives of their children is not new, especially in Northern India. The states of Punjab, Haryana, Uttar Pradesh, Bihar and Rajasthan are notorious for filial homicide. The problem is so rampant that the 242nd Report of Law Commission of India has reflected upon it and has specifically asked for a Bill to be introduced to this effect. At the time of writing this, a state Bill was passed on 6 August 2019 in Rajasthan.

One of the biggest observations I have had with regard to this is that there is a strong belief among village folk that this is the right thing to do. During my tenure as the Additional Solicitor General of India, I had the opportunity to observe this from all angles. While arguing a case by the name of Shakti Vahini, where the issue of diktats issued by the khap panchayats was being evaluated, I observed the vehemence and the belief that these organizations and individuals have towards the ideas of *gotra* or *jaat*. That an entire community holds the idea that women, or in several cases even men, are properties and extensions of their families is astounding. The fact remains that the idea of personal autonomy, which we in the urban or the so called 'educated' society so vehemently protect, does not exist.

It was a strange experience arguing about it, and it felt like I was arguing with someone who lives in ancient times. The truth of the matter is that when we look at it objectively, these rules of jaat and gotra might have a base in practicality, but we have to admit that today these ideals do not stand the test of time.

LESSONS AHEAD

The most ironical thing about honour killing is the fact that there is no 'honour' in killing. The increase in such crimes at an alarming rate is an apt illustration of the intolerance and patriarchal ethos embedded in the minds of people, which, if not changed, will lead to such disgraceful and abominable practices becoming the norm. Despite international humanitarian law proscribing any gender-based brutality, honour violence is committed across the world, often with impunity. Despite the widespread and severe nature of the violence, most cases remain unreported. Parliament of India is already in the process of drafting a Bill which will put honour killings under a separate heading of crime.[1]

The root cause for this menace is illiteracy. There is still a huge section of urban and rural population that identifies with the values of yore. Unfortunately, with the changing of times, some of these values become obsolete and it is a rigid adherence to these that creates violence and dissonance in contemporary society. Our yearning to follow the ways we have been taught since generations oftentimes overpowers our sense of right or wrong.

The Supreme Court has now given guidelines for the oft-dreaded khap panchayats, with regards to their diktats on honour killing. The Supreme Court has directed that any attempt by khap panchayats or any other assembly to scuttle or prevent two consenting adults from marrying is absolutely 'illegal', and has laid down preventive, remedial and punitive measures in this regard. The judiciary of this country has taken steps needed to eradicate this bizarre murder rite. However, it remains to be seen what we as a civil society do. Do we still allow our children to die for choosing their partner? Or do we respect their autonomy as individuals?

---

[1]Sharma, Vibha, 'Who gave khaps the right to kill: PC', *The Tribune*, 27 March 2010, https://tinyurl.com/4htadrjc. Accessed on 17 November 2023.

Enfants Terribles

Sanjay Dutt and TADA

'Fame is a fickle mistress', one hears this very often, especially in the corridors I move in, and there are none more famous in India than the ones who grace the silver screen.

All of us, me included, have grown up on a steady diet of cinema. Depending on what generation we belong to, our lives have somewhere been dictated by these heroes on screen, right from Raj Kapoor for my mother to Amitabh Bachchan for my generation and to the latest young guns of Indian cinema.

What our ideologies are, is often also reflected in the way we dress and act, or speak and behave. Legions of men in my university wore the classic bell-bottomed pants and shirts, emulating the angry young man. Women dressed and emulated who they liked and identified with, such as Asha Parekh and Hema Malini. Such is the allure of films; we laugh and we cry with the characters in these stories woven for us and crafted to reflect the world, sometimes true, and sometimes dystopian and fantastical.

Movies turn actors into almost demigods, especially in the Indian society. We love cinema, we love our actors and we have taken hero worship to a level where we build temples for them. What we often forget is that these are characters which are written by screenwriters, and the screen plays images of fantasy, not the truth. The actresses are often not the shy, coy women we see on screen, and many times the hero is not a hero in real life. What we see is fiction and it is played out by human beings who have the same follies as most of us, or maybe a bit more. The status that movie stars enjoy is almost unreal, but being human and fallible, when they fall from grace, it is an almost Icarus-like fall from the highs of adulation to the lows of ridicule.

Law and justice are often considered synonymous, with the expectation that the law serves justice and justice is administered within the bounds of the law. However, for some prominent individuals, these principles are manipulated, turning the law into a tool wielded by shrewd lawyers and judges to subvert justice. Lady Justice finds herself ensnared in procedural complexities or with the scales of evidence being manipulated. This dichotomy leads to contentious and intricate situations, especially when involving high-profile personalities. The resulting legal battles often become the focus of films, further elevating the status of the very individuals who were at the center of these cases, turning them into cult figures.

Recently, movies like *No One Killed Jessica* (2011) and *Sanju* (2018) have been released to massive fanfare. Some of the more famous cases have been Sanjay Dutt's riveting tryst with 'terrorism' and Salman Khan's horrendous liquor-charged massacre of sleeping pavement dwellers. These incidents have made it to the big screen either directly or indirectly.

I have a distinct memory of a Supreme Court judge, who, on noticing that the matter is a criminal case, upon being asked to 'quash' an FIR, in his inimitable style, would ask wryly, 'So Mr Counsel, is your client in the queue of R.K. Kapoor or in Bhajan Lal's category?'

For what we see, the demigods behind the cinema screen are, like us, fallible and insecure. As I was writing this, the case of the suicide of actor Sushant Singh Rajput had captured the attention of the entire country. The narrative is two-sided; on one hand, the media and a section of the populace were baying for the blood of an actress, who was supposedly the girlfriend of the deceased; on the other hand, the narrative had become an issue of feminism, asking questions of why can't a man be seen as having absolute control over his own actions.

Something that caught my eye was a picture being shared across some social media outlets. It was a side-by-side comparison of how some male actors who have been accused of crimes were treated and the way this actress was being treated. The photo showed both the male actors being escorted gracefully by the policemen, while this poor woman was hounded by the police and the incessant media.

Whether the affluent and renowned receive preferential treatment within our legal system hinges on the construction of the narrative surrounding their lives. I'm not asserting that they experience leniency, but rather, their constant exposure to the public eye amplifies the significance of their wrongdoings when they occur.

THE CURIOUS CASE OF SANJAY DUTT

Sanjay Dutt's life has almost legendary qualities to it. Born to superstars Sunil Dutt and Nargis Dutt, it's a story begging to be told with all its ebbs and flows. His life is now the subject of a Bollywood biopic, with its many twists and turns, and has been made for thrilling cinematic experience. The life of Sanjay Dutt has now been in the public eye for more than six decades. His notoriety stems from a variety of incidents, including his history of drug abuse, his stellar performances, his megastar parents, but most of all, his conviction under the Arms Act, for the possession of guns that were allegedly to be used in the infamous Bombay Blasts. Sanjay Dutt's case is an eye opener that shows us how the criminal justice system operates at different levels and for different people.

To try and understand why this was such a controversy, we need to understand what exactly the Terrorist and Disruptive Activities (Prevention) Act, or TADA, was. The Act was a historically controversial law, controversial not because it was easily manipulated, but because it was draconian in its operation. The law clearly outlined offenses, and the associated punishments were harsh and meted out swiftly from its inception in 1985.

The times were such that it demanded this law. Bombay, or Mumbai as it is now called, was reeling under the mafia's rule. It was the heyday of men like Dawood Ibrahim, and religious fanaticism had just taken hold of the country. India had opened its economy and it was a time for new beginnings, which also meant that the radicalization that existed outside India, for the first time, made forays into our society and was the precursor to what in time would be known all over the world as 'Islamic terrorism'. To counter this rising threat, we needed a law that was strong and mindful of what it wanted to achieve. That is not to say it was an unmindful law; it justified its ends because it was a legislation created to put a stop to terrorist activities.

The trial and procedure that followed in Sanjay Dutt's case went on to show that despite the law not leaving room for any ambiguity, it could still be manipulated. The charges levelled against Sanjay Dutt were principally 'abetment' and 'conspiracy' under TADA, and yet, despite an admitted confession, the trial court acquitted the man. Another extremely odd feature of the case was that there was no appeal filed against the acquittal by the incumbent central government. Now, it is conjecture whether this was a case of a man being acquitted because he and his father were in a position to exert substantial influence, or was it simply that the court believed him to be a wayward youth who was just doing the wrong thing at the wrong time.

Acquittals in law are an odd business, not because they prove guilt or innocence, but because they are never final. The other party almost always files an appeal, more so when the cases are of crimes which have had a significant impact. To illustrate the point, I have argued cases in the Supreme Court as the Additional Solicitor General for the Republic of India, for sums as low as ₹250, simply because the law involved was the Anti-Corruption Law. To give a background to this, we need to see why TADA was necessary and why Sanjay came to be embroiled in it.

The life of a movie star is very public, more so when he is a star kid. Sanjay Dutt's life was considered almost ideal. He was a budding film star in an India which was just spreading its wings. Youth was just awakening to the ideas of clubs and parties and drinking and drugs, and Sanjay Dutt was right in the middle of it.

This was also the India of the mafia. I've often heard that Dawood Ibrahim had a stranglehold on Bollywood, and a few, if not most, of the movies used to be mafia funded. This also meant arms and gang wars used to be routine in Mumbai, and this was also the subject of myriad movies that glamorized and idolized the mafia and its lifestyle.

What led to Sanjay Dutt being entangled in this web, and whether he was guilty or not, are subjects for the judiciary to contemplate. As a lawyer, I can only dare to look at what was presented, by the facts recorded and the trials that took place subsequently. Shorn of details, Sanjay Dutt returned to India in April 1993 from Mauritius, and was arrested at the airport itself under serious offences of TADA under which the minimum jail term is of a decade.

Accused of conspiracy and abetment in the 1993 Bombay Blasts Mr Dutt made an admission on 26 April 1993 and on 28 April 1993 at 4.00 p.m. before police officer K.C. Bishnoi. The confession was detailed and made after he had been arrested—it was, thus, admissible in law. It was this confession that clearly admitted Sanjay Dutt's involvement in terrorist activities that remained unrebutted for many years.

Sanjay Dutt was arrayed as 'accused no. 117' in Yakub Menon's TADA case, along with other accused persons before the Special Court constituted in Bombay. He was charged with conspiracy, whose objective had been to alienate sections of people and adversely affect the harmony of different sections of people and commit illegal acts by using explosives, bombs and firearms like AK-56 rifles, pistols and other lethal weapons.

The question here was why did he want to acquire arms. To get an insight into this question is where it gets murky. Sanjay Dutt was an actor who had proved himself well at that time, but this was also a man who had been through a lot in his life by that time. His mother, who by all accounts was very close to him, had passed away a few days before his first film released, which was a massive hit. So, while as an actor he was basking in the adulation, as a son he was grieving. This was also the time when he was by most accounts already addicted to various drugs and was active in the party circuit of Bombay. Like many young men who have both fame and grief, he had turned to drugs and had to be admitted to drug rehabs outside the country.

When he came back as a changed man, it was the time when the Babri Masjid demolition had happened. His father was a politician at that time, and had been active in the relief work at the time of the riots in Ayodhya and throughout the country. Sanjay Dutt had supposedly claimed in court that his father used to get death threats, and that was the reason he had wanted to acquire arms—to protect himself and his family. When I think about the motive for this young man, who had a Muslim mother and a Hindu father, to be embroiled in a situation which resulted in the Bombay Blasts, I admit, I become numb. There is a part of me which accepts that maybe he was just a young boy gone wayward, and had no intention to indulge in terrorist acts, or for that matter knew what his actions meant. I do state a caveat here to say that this is only my opinion, and the law does not take into account the intention.

Mr Dutt was in possession of firearms and allegedly had links with Dawood Ibrahim. The arms had supposedly been delivered to him in a very secret manner and he had accepted these deliveries. The law on terror was clear and cogently worded. Any person who is in unauthorized and conscious possession of a firearm as described under the Act, in a Notified Area (i.e., Bombay) in 1993, had to be dealt under TADA laws, which had longer jail terms than under the Arms Act. During the trial, the accused can, of course, defend and produce evidence which a prudent court would be willing to believe.

The criminal charges under TADA were clearly made out. Sanjay then proceeded further and recorded his confession. He was supposedly in contact with a member from Dawood Ibrahim's gang called Qayyum and he was offered a pistol, which he allegedly liked and bought. Thus, unfortunately, Sanjay Dutt supposedly had the requisite knowledge that he was collaborating with a known gang member of the Dawood Ibrahim gang. The charge and the evidence under the Terror Laws was complete. In the normal course of events, Sanjay should have been convicted under the Terror Laws.

Accused no. 41 Musa Chauhan was Sanjay Dutt's friend. He, too, in his unchallenged confession, deposed that Anees Ibrahim was a notorious smuggler, and when the Hingora brothers had come to Sanjay Dutt's home, the film star had himself seen AK-56 rifles being removed from the hidden cavity of the car. A cache of firearms was being taken out in the garage of his home in his presence. The law says that if one sees something illegal happening, one is bound by the law to inform the police. Not informing then becomes a cognizable offence for which a common man can be arrested and jailed.

Sanjay Dutt also supposedly confessed, that he had lied to his father Sunil Dutt about the acquisition of AK-56 rifles. Sanjay Dutt had a true friend named Yusuf Nulwalla. As a true friend, he did whatever his friend wanted him to do. He was instructed by Sanjay, over a phone call from Mauritius, to go to this home and destroy the incriminating and explosive fire arms. He picked up the stuff, which was in a black bag, from his second floor hall. He deposed that Sanjay felt that the Hingoras will sing like canaries and will divulge his involvement, so he told his friend to get rid of the arms. Sanjay was released on bail, whereas this friend, who had destroyed the rifles on his instruction, was denied any such liberty. Justice is indeed blind! Yusuf was accused no. 118.

Yusuf deposed in court that he cut the AK-56 rifle into pieces, and put all the pieces back into the bag, and induced his friend who was in the steel fabrication business to aid his friend, Sanjay, by eliminating all traces by the use of a gas cutter.

The pistol, too, bought from the gang of Dawood Ibrahim, was burnt at the site and melted. A part of AK-56 rifle was thrown into Marine Drive, where today the Oberoi Towers stand. The bullets, too, were wrapped into separate bundles and were thrown into the Arabian Sea.

The idea was simple. Sanjay Dutt was a player in a much bigger agenda to destabilize the government and the Republic of India. The weapons that were given to him on 18 January 1993 were to be used in a bigger sequence of events. Almost like the movies he acts in, the trajectory of events that transpired in 1993 forever changed the face of India, and have had immense ramifications—both politically and emotionally—for the citizens of this country. The Bombay Blasts rocked the already smouldering city on 12 March 1993 and was considered by many to be the retribution for the Babri Masjid demolition. The suppliers and the persons involved in the Bombay Blasts were all charged under TADA terrorist laws under Section 3 and Section 5 of the Act and were all sentenced to long-term imprisonment.

The confession, of not only Sanjay Dutt, but confessions of accused no. 53 Samir Hingora, accused no. 41 Madhu Chauhan, accused no. 89 Manzoor Ahmed, accused no. 118 Mohsin Nulwalla, as well as confession of Bapuj Adjania, who produced the spring of the rod of AK-56 rifle from his foundry, all corroborated with each other substantially. All of them were believed by all the courts as 'true and voluntarily' and were accepted under Section 15 of TADA.

The chain of evidence was thus complete. When the trial had well begun, a competent lawyer whispered to Sanjay Dutt, that his other lawyers had completely forgotten to advise him to retract the 'confession', as otherwise it would blow his cover. Like a tacky Bollywood detective film, it was retracted, but the damage had already been done. The courts disbelieved his retraction and held to be false, and the confession was recorded as true and voluntarily.

Not only was Sanjay an abettor, but allegedly an equal partner to the crime as the evidence of other co-accused was believed by all the courts in which it was deposed that 'hand grenades' had been kept in his car and Samir had left his car in the garage of Sanjay Dutt. AK-56 supplier Samir had himself taken an auto rickshaw from 58 Palli Hill, home of Sanjay Dutt, while his own Maruti Van had remained at Sanjay Dutt's home for three days in his garage. It was the same van from which the lethal weapons had been taken out.

During the search for the truth during the trial, the prosecution seemed to have no steam, and no interest at all to prosecute Sanjay under Terror Laws and carry the same to its logical end, even though the facts were glaring!

Sanjay Dutt was acquitted of terror charges, and the state government chose not to file an appeal. However, he was able to secure bail after 18 months of imprisonment. Eleven years later, the TADA court acquitted him of all charges after making an observation that he was not a terrorist and had acquired the guns for self-defence. He was then convicted under the Arms Act and sentenced to six years in jail, which he had managed to secure a bail for from the Supreme Court. He was sent to the Yerwada prison in Pune on 31 July 2007. However, he was later let out on bail several times. His term was then further cut short to five years by the Supreme Court on 21 March 2013. I leave it to the reader to draw their own inference whether the prosecution went backwards to protect the child of a famous film personality.

Mr Dutt, when he was given a lighter jail sentence and a year was waived off by the Supreme Court, remained undeterred on trying to seek more favours. He hired a top-notch lawyer who pleaded that his client be given a longer period to surrender to jail; he got a reprieve of a month.

The new form of TADA is Unlawful Activities (Prevention) Act, and today it has become almost synonymous with our lives. We hear it very often. I would say that times have changed along with the sensibilities of our population. The terror of insurgency is at our doorstep and has been recruiting children as young as 10 years through social media. Everybody has a phone these days, and everybody has a social media account and sometimes, unfortunately for us, it just takes one wrong video or a cleverly placed smooth talk to lead our children on a path from which few return like Mr Dutt. The New Criminal Bills seem to have been awaken to this reality and have incorporated terrorist activities as a part of the larger spectrum of the Penal Code applicable pan India, rather than as specialized Acts made by states.

I Am Woman

Bhanwari Devi and Sexual Harassment Law

'I am woman, hear me roar
In numbers too big to ignore'

—Helen Reddy

I heard the song 'I Am Woman' by chance, in a movie called *Sex and the City 2* (2010), where Sarah Jessica Parker and her three girlfriends go to Abu Dhabi on a girls' trip. The song, I later came to know, was released in 1972, the time I was growing up in the by-lanes of Old Delhi.

The lyrics struck me and reminded me of the world I grew up in. In the traditions of Old Delhi, for families that came from Punjab, women seemed to have their own language. It was understood that they go through tremendous hardships in their lives to gain even the smallest of things. We as a generation have seen a monumental shift in the status and the accessibility of women. While our mothers and grandmothers were barely educated, our daughters have access that older generations could not even have dreamt of.

In the '70s, when Helen Reddy was singing this song, India was still in the middle of rediscovering its strength. As a democracy born merely a quarter of a century ago, we were still grappling to come to terms with fine-tuning our society.

While the women in the West were trying to 'roar', we, the women of India, were still trying to discover if we could. It was the ultimate coming of age for Indian women; we were looking at expanding boundaries, and getting out of our homes and hearths to try and create our own careers and break glass ceilings.

All this and many more developments were taking place, no doubt. But any woman who has lived through that time would tell you, patriarchy remained. The success stories were there, but they were the exceptions rather than the rule, and although women were trying to come into their own, there were several hurdles—ones that often looked like male chauvinism and the restrictiveness of patriarchy. The cruelest and the vilest amongst them is sexual dominance and aggression. Raping and assaulting women, just for men to prove their power over them.

On 20 March 2020, the country got together even as it was fighting the scariest of pandemics and amidst the implementation of the social distancing, to revel and rejoice at the early morning execution of the four men convicted of the gangrape and murder in the infamous Nirbhaya gang-rape case. The accused tried everything in the book to delay their execution by filing various petitions, curative petitions, going back and forth between forums and, in fact, were successful in their attempts on two occasions, but as they say: 'Truth always triumphs'. The morning was greeted with posters that read 'morning of justice' and 'thanks to judiciary', which were seen in huge numbers even in the wee hours of the morning outside Tihar Jail, where the accused were executed. While one daughter of the country finally got justice, this chapter is dedicated to the one, who in her own words, has not got justice from the court but from the people in the country; the protagonist and the force behind the law pertaining to sexual harassment in the workplace—Bhanwari Devi or Bhori Devi.

In India, the discussion on the topic of sexual harassment in the workplace dates back to 1997, when, in what is often quoted as the finest example of judicial activism, the Supreme Court laid down the Vishakha Guidelines, in the landmark judgment of *Vishaka and Others v. State of Rajasthan and Others.* The guidelines, in turn, laid down the foundation for the Sexual Harassment of Women at Workplace (Prevention, Prohibition and Redressal) Act, 2013.

However, why did we need the Vishakha Guidelines is a story which makes us both weep at the tragedy and feel pride at the power of a woman who took up arms. The story is of 1992, when I was around 30 years of age and had just started coming into my own as a lawyer, and my personal quest for women's rights had just begin to take a hold on me. The life of Bhanwari Devi became a living example of how women 'roar' and the power of their voices that today, after more than quarter of a century, can still be heard.

She was merely 6 years old, at a time when kids were learning to play with new toys, Bhanwari Devi, or Bhori Devi was married. Her village in Rajasthan, around 34 kilometres from Jaipur, practiced child marriage and she had been a six-year-old child bride. Strange as it was, it led to a radical change in Bhanwari Devi. Rather than submitting to the age-old custom as 'the accepted thing', even as a young child, she evaluated it and realized the perils. She didn't rebel against her own marriage, but decided that she didn't want others to be subjected to this evil, and so in the year 1985, she joined the Women Development Programme run by the Rajasthan state government as a 'saathin' to work towards the prevention of child marriage by not only creating awareness among people but also reporting such incidents to the concerned authorities. In 1992, she became aware of an impending marriage of a nine-month-old baby belonging to a high-caste community in her village. As a child bride herself, she understood what being one meant, and to stop the marriage, she went to the house to counsel the family against such a decision. However, all her efforts went in vain as on the next day, the family got the baby married.

Defiance from a woman belonging to a low caste irked the family and the villagers. As punishment for her actions, she was shunned by the village and was denied all services, even by her community. On 22 September 1992, Bhanwari Devi was allegedly gang-raped by five members of the high-caste Gujjar community in the presence of her husband. 'I was just doing my job. She was a nine-month child and I had to stop it. I had to report it to the police. I spoke to the family and they refused to listen. I was abused and thrown out,' Bhanwari recalled in an interview.[1] The Bhanwari Devi case revealed the perils of sexual assault at workplace, which millions of working women were exposed to across the country, and also portrayed the extent to which harm can be caused if the problem is not nipped in the bud.

As is unfortunately a tale too common, the police did not take Bhanwari Devi's complaint seriously and it took a herculean effort to even get an FIR registered. The only male doctor available at the primary health centre refused to conduct her medical examination. She had to travel to Jaipur to get her medical examination done, where, due to the unavailability of the Magistrate, her medical examination was further delayed. After 52 hours, her medical test was conducted, which should have been done within 24 hours. In the report, her scratches and bruises were not recorded and her complaints of physical discomfort were ignored. It was more than a year after the crime when the five accused were finally arrested, and were charged

---

[1]Kedia, Shruti, 'Meet the Woman Whose Lifelong Struggle Laid the Foundation for Laws against Sexual Harassment in the Workplace', *YourStory,* 8 January 2018, https://bit.ly/3ugwXwC. Accessed on 1 December 2022.

with harassment, assault, conspiracy and gang rape.

Throughout the trial, judges were inexplicably changed five times. She was taunted and humiliated at every step. In the year 1995, the trial court in Rajasthan acquitted all five men accused of raping Bhanwari Devi on the grounds of inadequacy of evidence. The trial court convicted the accused only for offences such as conspiracy and assault, thereby subjecting them to imprisonment for a period of nine months, which only added insult to the injury.

The verdict of the trial court led to a huge outcry among various women groups across the country. Protest rallies were held in different parts of the country and the government of Rajasthan was forced to file an appeal against the decision of the trial court. Even after the passage of more than twenty-eight years of the incident, the appeal in the matter is yet to see the light of the day, when two of the five accused are already dead.

In a recent interview, when Bhanwari Devi was told that her story has inspired a generation of woman, she said, 'If at all you find my story inspiring, don't just stop there. Empowerment is not just about listening and knowing about injustice; it is also about speaking up and acting on it.' Talking about her quest for justice, she said, 'I am not afraid. What more can they do? I am not alone in my fight. The justice and the case is not just about me anymore. I am fighting for a society where there is gender equality; where there is no discrimination between two siblings of a household; where both brother and sister get equal rotis and education opportunities.' She also expressed her displeasure towards the judicial system and said: 'The court of law and the government has failed me but I got justice in the people's court.'[2]

The major issue that cropped up in Bhanwari Devi's case was

---

[2]Ibid.

that the Government of Rajasthan had refused to own up to the fact that she was attacked while she was on duty for the Women Development Programme. The state government had taken a stand that Ms Bhanwari Devi had been raped while working in the field with her husband and not while performing her duties as saathin.

The state's failure to recognize Ms Bhanwari Devi as their worker or the fact that she had to suffer the worst form of sexual aggression for her actions taken during her employment exposed the hazards faced by working women on a daily basis, and the need was felt to fill the vacuum that existed in the sphere of formation of rules to safeguard women's rights in the workplace. Accordingly, Vishakha, an NGO established for rights-based intervention in the area of education, health and combating violence against women, and other organizations, such as the Women's Rehabilitation Group from Rajasthan, Jagori and Kali for Women from Delhi approached the Supreme Court of India by way of Public Interest Litigation (PIL), in 1992, seeking that acts of sexual harassment be recognized as a violation of a women's fundamental right to equality, and that all workplaces be made accountable and responsible to uphold these rights.

The then Solicitor General of India, late Sh. T.R. Andhyarujina, appeared for the Respondent, Union of India, and Shri Fali S. Nariman was appointed amicus curiae in the case. They rendered constructive and valuable insights and assistance to help attain the most reasonable and just outcome to the issue at hand having profuse and substantial implications. The judgment passed by a three-judge bench comprising the then Chief Justice of India Justice J.S. Verma, Justice Sujata V. Manohar and Justice B.N. Kirpal on 13 August 1997 displayed candour and sensitivity. This was a judgment that is one of the best examples of judicial activism. The court committed itself to formulate the guidelines in order to provide an effective redressal mechanism to curb the violation of the integral rights of women and was done in the absence of any legislative measures in order to address the pressing need for preventing women from being exposed to such perils at their workplace.

'It was a revolutionary judgment based on the fundamental rights of women. The guidelines later became the basis for a 2013 law passed by the Indian Parliament to prevent sexual harassment of women at the workplace. Bhanwari Devi had no direct role in this law, but she was the catalyst for this, she was the main factor. She is a very brave woman,' stated Prof Renuka Pamecha, a Jaipur-based women's rights activist, in an interview.[3]

The Supreme Court laid down the law, which was unconventional and unique since the court had drawn a remarkable reference to international law and the fundamental rights of an individual envisaged in the Constitution of India, thereby concluding that sexual harassment in the workplace causes grave violation of the human rights of women, the fundamental rights of gender equality and the Right to Life, the right to live with dignity included therein, and personal liberty embodied under Article 14, Article 15 and Article 21 of the Constitution of India. Moreover, the court opined that Bhanwari Devi's case also depicted an infringement of the fundamental right of the victim 'to practice any profession or to carry out any occupation, trade or business' provided for under Article 19 (1)(g), which, in turn, largely depends upon the availability of a safe, hazard-free, favourable and conducive work environment. To quote late Chief Justice J.S. Verma, who authored the judgment: 'The meaning and content of the fundamental rights guaranteed in the Constitution

[3]Pandey, Geeta, 'Bhanwari Devi: The rape that led to India's sexual harassment law', *BBC*, 17 March 2017, https://tinyurl.com/yef96ana. Accessed on 1 December 2022.

of India are of sufficient amplitudes to encompass all facets of gender equality.'

The Supreme Court, while holding that gender equality includes protection from sexual harassment, and the right to work with dignity, went ahead and defined what acts/behaviour may amount to sexual harassment, which it decided includes any such unwelcome sexually determined behaviour.

The definition was broad enough and covered situations where a woman could be in a position of disadvantage in her workplace as a result of threats relating to employment decisions that could negatively affect her working life. The other feature of the guidelines to prevent sexual harassment at the workplace was a duty cast upon all the employers or persons in charge to take appropriate steps to prevent sexual harassment.

The employer is also duty-bound to ensure that victims or witnesses are not victimized or discriminated against while dealing with complaints of sexual harassment. The victims of sexual harassment were given the option to seek transfer of the offender or their own transfer. The employer was cast with the obligation to take appropriate disciplinary action against the offender in case the conduct of offender amounts to misconduct in employment as defined by the relevant service rules.

The court recommended the creation of a complaint mechanism in the organization which would look into the complaint made by the victim and decide whether or not such conduct constitutes an offence under law or a breach of the service rules in a time-bound manner. The complaints committee had to be headed by a woman and it was mandated that not less than half of its members be women. Whilst holding that the proceedings before the complaint committee are confidential, the court, to prevent the possibility of any undue pressure or influence from senior levels, laid down that such complaints committees should involve a third party, either an NGO or other bodies that are familiar with the issue of sexual harassment.

The employees, on the other hand, were given the right to raise issues of sexual harassment at workers' meetings and at other appropriate forums. The Supreme Court further directed that awareness should be created among women employees about their rights in the workplace. The Supreme Court also covered the grey area that was highlighted in Bhanwari Devi's case, where the offenders had not been her fellow workers but people belonging to a high-caste community in the area. The Supreme Court cast an obligation upon the employer or person in-charge to take all steps necessary and reasonable to assist the victim and take preventive measures where sexual harassment occurs as a result of an act by any third party or outsider.

Importantly, the guidelines laid down by the Supreme Court were in addition to the remedies already available under the Protection of Human Rights Act, 1993. The topmost court of the country held that the guidelines were to be regarded as 'law' within the meaning of Article 141 of the Constitution of India.

Currently, the guidelines hold historical and academic significance since they led to the enactment of an Act of Parliament on the subject in the year 2013, after a period of almost 16 years since they were first laid down by the Supreme Court.

DEVELOPMENT OF LAW POST THE VISHAKHA JUDGMENT

It was only 10 years after the formulation of the Vishaka Guidelines by the Supreme Court, that the first draft of the Protection of Women against Sexual Harassment at Workplace Bill, 2007, was prepared. I was the expert member on behalf of

National Commission for Women in the committee constituted for the drafting of the Bill, and even though the current law is hugely based on the guidelines laid by the Supreme Court, it is crucial that the law on the subject implements itself in the spirit as it was drafted.

Almost 16 years after laying down of the Vishakha Guidelines, the Indian legislation on the subject was promulgated and the Sexual Harassment of Women at Workplace (Prevention, Prohibition and Redressal) Act, 2013, was enacted by the Ministry of Women and Child Development in India as the country's first legislation specifically addressing the issue of sexual harassment at workplaces. The enactment aims at the protection and prevention of women from sexual harassment and provides for an effective redressal mechanism of complaints thereof. Under the Act, employers are expected to have a no-tolerance policy towards sexual harassment and have a policy that:

- prohibits any form of sexual harassment;
- prevents occurrence of any incident of sexual harassment by sensitizing the employees and by conducting awareness sessions;
- and provides a detailed framework for redressal.

The first question that comes to mind is what actions amount to sexual harassment as per the Sexual Harassment of Women at Workplace (Prevention, Prohibition and Redressal) Act, also known as the POSH Act. The Act used the definition of sexual harassment propounded by the Supreme Court in the Vishakha judgment. The definition of 'sexual harassment' given under the POSH Act is wide enough to cover both implied as well as explicit acts and behaviour of sexual harassment, which may be physical, verbal or written. Further, the said acts of sexual harassment by the perpetrator are unwanted and uncalled for by the victim. A person who is in a dominant position, pressurizes any of his female co-workers for quid pro quo, i.e. sexual favours in lieu of job promotion, threat or taking detrimental actions against them. The casting couch in the film industry is the best-known example of quid pro quo. While some forms of sexual harassment like sexual assault are invasive, and an isolated act may be treated as sexual harassment, some other forms of sexual harassment may not be distinguishable easily but may lead to a hostile work environment for the victim. It is imperative to remember, however, that sexual harassment at the workplace is unwelcomed and the experience is subjective. It is the impact and not the intent that matters and it is normally seen that sexual harassment occurs in a background where power rests with the harasser. The Delhi High Court, in the matter of *Dr. Punita K. Sodhi v. Union of India* recognized the fact that sexual harassment is a subjective experience and held:

> We therefore prefer to analyse harassment from the complainant's perspective. [...] Men tend to view some forms of sexual harassment as 'harmless social interactions to which only overtly sensitive women would object. The characteristically male view depicts sexual harassment as comparatively harmless amusement [...] Men, who are rarely victims of sexual assault may view sexual conduct in a vacuum without a full appreciation of the social setting or the underlying threat of violence that a woman may perceive.

THE ME TOO MOVEMENT

The inception of the 'Me Too' movement, which has taken the world by storm, dates back to the year 2006, when Tarana J. Burke, the founder and executive director of the movement, incepted the idea for the purpose of offering help to survivors of sexual harassment and a way for young people to share their stories. Subsequently, their work expanded in leaps and bounds and reached survivors in the global community and persons belonging to various walks of life, thereby bringing about a movement at the global level, leading to combating stigmatization and throwing light upon the widespread impact of sexual violence worldwide.

The movement started to gain momentum and limelight when, in the year 2017, former American film producer and one of the most powerful faces of Hollywood, Harvey Weinstein, was accused by various actresses of propositioning and assaulting them while pursuing acting roles in films. Consequently, the movement started to encourage various survivors to voice their stories as they found unanimity and cohesion in the global movement; additionally, a few victims also resorted to seeking legal action against the perpetrators to hold them liable. The movement highlights the severity and graveness of the incidents of sexual harassment, occurring in different countries and locations across the globe, and in varying degrees. The massive publicity obtained by the movement has stimulated and led to the uplifting of women when they disclosed stories of the unwelcomed and inappropriate conduct they had been subjected to, and which consequently resulted in the conviction of various offenders. Contrarily, it has also been contended that the widespread movement on social media platforms has resulted in false accusations with the intent to defame or with a motive to harm the other party.

In the year 2002, allegations of sexual harassment were levelled against Phaneesh Murthy, who had become the director of Infosys in the year 2000, by his former secretary. Infosys allegedly settled the lawsuit out of court for a certain amount of money and fired Murthy in 2002.

In the year 2013, Tarun Tejpal, a high-profile journalist, was accused of rape and sexual harassment by a woman colleague. The incident took place during the Think Festival that was being hosted by Tehelka at a five-star hotel in Goa's Bambolim in 2013, when the junior colleague was allegedly assaulted inside a lift. While the trial is still pending, the Supreme Court dismissed Tejpal's petition to quash the FIR lodged against him.

In the year 2015, a woman who used to work with R.K. Pachauri at The Energy and Resources Institute (TERI), a Delhi-based energy and environment research centre, filed a complaint against him. She claimed that Pachauri had flooded her with offensive messages, emails and texts and made several 'carnal and perverted' advances over the 16 months they had worked together. Accordingly, on 18 February 2015, Delhi Police filed an FIR against Pachauri on allegations of sexual harassment, stalking and criminal intimidation. Further, in May 2015, the Internal Committee (IC) of TERI, after examining over 50 employees, found Pachauri guilty of sexual harassment. The recommendations of the IC of TERI were challenged before the Industrial Tribunal on the grounds of violation of the principles of natural justice, which stayed the recommendations of IC. An article stating an account of sexual harassment suffered by the woman employees of TERI by the hands of Mr Pachauri was published in the Indian magazine *The Caravan*.[4] Consequently, the district court in Saket, New Delhi, framed charges of molestation against the accused under Section 355, Section 354A and Section 509 of the IPC. Mr Pachauri died on 13 February 2020, while the matter was still in court.

In the year 2018, Binny Bansal, co-founder of Flipkart, was forced to tender his resignation after allegations of sexual

---

[4]Saxena, Nikita, 'How RK Pachauri Systematically Harassed Women at TERI', *The Caravan*, 7 November 2017, https://bit.ly/3XRbNTE. Accessed on 1 December 2022.

harassment were levelled against him by a subordinate female employee. One of the most prominent cases pertaining to the Me Too movement in our country involves Priya Ramani, a journalist based in Bangalore, who levelled allegations of sexual misconduct and harassment against former Union Minister M.J. Akbar in the year 2018 by tweeting and addressing him as 'the unidentified man', referred to in an article titled 'To the Harvey Weinsteins of the World', authored by her for *Vogue*, where she describes her job interview with M.J. Akbar. Consequently, her tweet set off a surge of accusations by various other journalists against the accused, which, in turn, led to the resignation of the politician from the designation of the Minister of State for External Affairs. He, however, denied all the accusations. Following this, he brought a suit against Ramani for criminal defamation and contended that she had defamed him with full knowledge that her conduct would cause harm to his reputation. The defamation suit filed by Akbar asserts that as a journalist, Ramani is vested with more responsibility and was aware of the consequences of her conduct. The matter is still sub judice and would eventually be a landmark decision on whether the movement is being used judicially and helping women speak up now after having suffered harassment several years ago, or if it is only being used as a tool to settle personal scores.

Indian comedian Utsav Chakraborty was one of the foremost persons to be accused of sexual misconduct on social media platforms in October 2018. Amongst others, claims were imposed against him by writer Mahima Kukreja, who asserted that the comedian had sent her unsolicited intimate images about two years ago.

William Shakespeare's play *Measure for Measure*, written four centuries ago and set in the Catholic city of Vienna, comes to my mind as a part of the play appears to be similar to a story pertaining to the Me Too movement. The play commences with the Duke of Vienna temporarily stepping down from his post and vesting the responsibility over Angelo, his ultra-virtuous deputy. Following the arrest of Claudio, who had impregnated his lover, Isabella, his sister and a pivotal character in the play, seeks mercy from Angelo, who, in turn, asks her for sexual favours in return for Claudio's life. Subsequently, Isabella confronts Angelo to seek pardon on behalf of her brother, and states that if her brother is not excused, she would reveal the true character of Angelo to the world. Angelo reverts with a startling remark and states, 'Who will believe thee, Isabel?' Shakespeare, by the use of the famous quote, draws an inference to the prevalence of the imbalance of power between men and the women and the difference in authority vested in them. He further wrote 'My false o'erweighs your true.' Angelo reminds Isabella of his status and that his word means more than hers: 'My unsoil'd name, the austereness of my life.' Angelo knows that if Isabella comes forward, it would ruin her chastity and even if she doesn't sleep with him, she'll have lost her reputation. Even after four centuries, *Measure for Measure* is still relevant in the present scenario.[5] In most of the cases of sexual harassment, the perpetrator is usually in the position of power, and the victim, despite no fault of her own, is subject to discrimination and a hostile environment in the workplace.

Today, the issue of sexual harassment at the workplace continues to remain a pervasive and a vehement attribute of patriarchy. However, in recent times, we've seen a commendable rise in the number of female achievers who have, as they say, 'broken the glass ceiling' and the same is evident from the far-reaching and widespread influx of women from different walks of life in

---

[5]Shakespeare, William, 'Measure for Measure', *Shakespeare-Online*, https://tinyurl.com/mv49kwvu. Accessed on 27 November 2023.

the industry. In this regard, The Ministry of Women and Child Development launched an online platform named 'SHe-Box' in the year 2017, as an acronym for Sexual Harassment Electronics Box, for the purpose of addressing grievances of women in regards to complaints of sexual harassment at workplaces, wherein government as well as private-sector employees can file complaints. This initiative is in furtherance of the aims and purposes of The Prevention of the Sexual Harassment at Workplace Act and provides for single-window access to every woman, regardless of whether she is employed in the organized or the unorganized sector, and enables women to register complaints through the online portal, following which the complaint is directly sent to the competent authority having jurisdiction to take action. As of December 2019, a total number of 203 cases had been disposed of by SHe-Box, which includes cases under the central government, state government and private sector.

Today, more than a quarter of a century after Bhanwari Devi first cried for equal rights and women empowerment, the 'roar' of this woman reached everywhere, and the change that she has brought in the lives of women is incomparable to any other in the recent history of modern India. This was the story of how Bhanwari Devi, a low-caste child bride from a village in Rajasthan taught all the women in India how to 'roar'.

What Is Love?

Section 377

The human tendency to conform to established norms is manifest. It doesn't matter whether we brutalize, vilify, or condemn a section of society for no fault of theirs. We classify identities as black and white, male or female, and condemn to wilderness those who cannot be contained in these straitjacket categories that emerge from our somewhat animalistic tendency to form social groups. A conspicuous illustration of this is our treatment and identification of the 'third gender' people as outcasts to be feared at the least or ridiculed. How wrong were we?

THE RIGHT OF UNION

As human beings, one of the basic instincts we hold dearest to us is the idea of freedom. Myriad cultures have different ideas of what freedom means—to some, it might mean freedom from foreign rule, as seen from rebellions across the world; and to some, these freedoms are more personal, like the freedom to worship their gods or the freedom to love whoever we choose, male or female, or what Chief Justice Misra subtly calls 'right of union'.

An essential facet of our lives is love. It starts to affect our lives the moment we are born—our mothers, then families form our first bonds of love, and then slowly, as we age, it diversifies. The idea of a romantic relationship fuels a furious imagination and is easily one of the driving forces in human life. We see poetry, songs and movies written on it. Epics are sung in the name of love. The human desire to share life with those they find attractive has both sparked conflicts and catalysed transformative events in history. In my era, gender was a binary concept, devoid of the fluidity and neutrality that contemporary discourse now acknowledges. I hail from a time when stoicism was expected of men, while women were granted the freedom to express their emotions.

Upon the initiation of discussions surrounding LGBTQIA+ matters in our nation, my initial reaction was one of profound astonishment. Such dialogues were conspicuously absent from our societal discourse. But times have changed, and constitutional morality as we interpret has changed. Today, thankfully, the debate is varied. It would be reductive to view constitutional morality as not a concept of its era. A constitutional expert examining the Constitution in 1951 would struggle to fathom a Constitution that would deem a 'right of union' as an essential tenet of Article 21 of Right to Life and Personal Liberty. That expert's imagination that qualifies their interpretation is limited by normative values of that society. Constitutional morality, despite its popular understanding as an objective principle-based framework of basic values that form an intrinsic part of constitutional identity, is limited in interpretation by the basic concept of human imagination. The mere ability to imagine a right emerging from constitutional morality is subject to our social values. It is in that spirit—I decided to understand what it meant to be in the LGBTQIA+ community in India. The research shocked me. I encountered harrowing accounts of men subjected to ghastly gang rapes and brutal assaults involving the merciless deployment of bricks. I was appalled to read about communal rapes, disturbingly endorsed by entire communities as a misguided attempt to 'cure' afflicted women, perpetrating a most nightmarish form of violence, often instigated by their own kin. I was further disheartened by the distressing accounts of unrepentant honour crimes, committed solely to shield families from what was perceived as an unnatural orientation.

As inhabitants of the Indian subcontinent, we have been nurtured within the confines of conservative societal constructs. It is worth noting that I do not cast aspersions on the environments that have fostered our development, as they have extended a significant measure of support to individuals, often surpassing what is available in ostensibly 'freer' societies. However, an unavoidable consequence of this nurturing has been the pervasive influence of our society on our individual choices. Throughout the passage of time, certain behaviors have acquired the taint of taboo, and regrettably, homosexuality has fallen under the shadow of societal censure.

As we cast our retrospective gaze upon the historical tapestry of homosexuality in India, it becomes evident that numerous episodes exist where not only was homosexuality tolerated, but it was indeed exalted and embraced. It would appear that our society had previously assimilated and celebrated these nuances in human choice with remarkable acceptance. The question that looms large is, where did our trajectory deviate from this path?

It is crucial to underscore that the concept of homosexuality extends beyond mere sexual interactions; it encompasses the profound dimensions of romantic love that transcend the realm of the physical. The connection between a romantic pair transcends the confines of sexual categorization, embracing the complexity of human relationships that defy facile compartmentalization, whether it pertains to bisexuality or transgender identities.

Instances of homophobia are prevalent throughout cultures, 'effeminate' boys are told to 'be a a man', and 'manly women' are told to act more like a lady. Some of the instances of homophobic rage that I have come across involve gang rapes, lynching and murder of these individuals. They could not go to the police or friends or family for fear of being outed. It is these individuals, the forgotten percentage of our society, that we need to protect and acknowledge.

Homosexuality seemed to have been accepted as a part of society in various time periods, not only in India but also across several parts of the world. The Greeks had a system called 'Pederasty', where a young boy was taken under the guidance of an older man, who introduced him to the society. Within this system, sex between men was acceptable. From Greco-Roman culture to the Persian, homosexuality seemed to have been accepted as a part of several societies. The gap in thought arose with the rise of Christianity, where the church interpreted scriptures to declare homosexuality as a sin

The imposition of Section 377 on the Indian colony of the British domain was legislated in 1861. At a time when Britain was colonizing most of the world, the law against homosexuality was introduced by the British in all its colonies, including Singapore, where it existed until it was decriminalized on 30 November 2022. Homosexuality had carried a fine and a life-term prison sentence.

With time, western countries accepted the concept of homosexuality. Today, all over the world, civil partnerships and marriages are the norm. However, the battle for sexual identification for Indian citizens was long pending. India's struggle for recognition of its LGBTQIA+ community started around 31 years ago, in 1991. When the virulent AIDS virus gripped the world, various groups were formed to create awareness for the patients afflicted with HIV. One organization called AIDS Bhedbhav Virodhi Andolan (ABVA), published an article detailing the extent of torture, blackmail and atrocities faced by the gay community in India. However, when the article was tabled at the Press Club of India, it was removed.

Three years later, another incident ignited a contentious dispute, as the then Inspector General of Police (IG) overseeing Tihar Jail adamantly declined to distribute condoms to the incarcerated denizens, ostensibly on the grounds of discouraging sexual relations between inmates. It was this very action that prompted the filing of a writ petition in the hallowed precincts of the Delhi High Court, beseeching not only for the provision of free condoms but also the annulment of Section 377 as constitutionally impermissible. This petition, however, languished in the judicial labyrinth, meeting its dismissal by the High Court seven years later.

The conundrum that unfolded left me pondering the paradoxical nature of withholding sexual protection from inmates in a bid to curtail the practice of homosexuality. It bore significant weight, as it signified an implicit acknowledgment of the existence of homosexual activities to the extent that the IG felt compelled to take preventive measures. This decisive action by the IG acted as the catalyst that reignited a simmering volcano, one that was on the precipice of being addressed, ushering forth a movement that ultimately paved the way for the decriminalization of same-sex relationships.

In 2001, an NGO by the name of Naz Foundation, an organization for HIV advocacy, petitioned the Delhi High Court calling for the striking down of Section 377. The movement against 377 had been gaining ground in India, but the final catalyst was a young man who ran terrified into the offices of The Naz Foundation. He told a gruesome story of how his parents had forced him into electroshock therapy to try and 'cure' him. Three years later, this petition was dismissed too. It was then that Naz Foundation filed a Special Leave Petition in the Supreme Court in February 2006.

The Supreme Court reinstated the case in the Delhi High Court because it was an issue of public interest. In the following months, Voices Against 377, a coalition of NGOs, joined the petition while India's Ministry of Home Affairs filed an affidavit against the decriminalization.

The Delhi High Court, in July 2009, held that Section 377 violated the fundamental Right to Life, liberty and equality. This was, however, overturned by the Supreme Court three years later, observing that Section 377 'does not suffer from the vice of unconstitutionality, and the declaration [...] of the High Court is legally unsustainable'.

From June 2016, events began speeding up towards its eventual repeal. Navtej Singh Johar, an award-winning Bharatanatyam dancer, and four other high-profile personalities filed a writ petition in the Supreme Court challenging Section 377. The nine-judge bench that heard the petition in August 2017 ruled that privacy is a fundamental right, sparking hope in activists and community members that change was around the corner.

More high-profile individuals joined the campaign, and in July 2018, a five-judge Supreme Court bench, which included Chief Justice Misra, began hearing the petitions against Section 377. Two months later came the historic verdict.

The day 6 September was eventful. India, for the first time, merged the two ideas of 'love' and 'identity' and, in doing so, did away with 150-year-old Victorian morality. It was on this day that we decided to let go of the archaic notions of homosexuality as being unnatural and gave precedence to our identity and the freedom of choice that our constitution promises.

Chief Justice Misra in a landmark tangent from the oft-taken Victorian moral views, opined,

> ...with the passage of time and evolution of the society, procreation is not the only reason for which people choose to come together. It is the choice of two consenting adults to perform sex for procreation or otherwise and if their choice is that of the latter, it cannot be said to be against the order of the nature. Therefore, sex performed differently, as per the choice of the consenting adults, does not per se make it against the order of the nature.

Another fascinating facet of this judgment was the prevalence of HIV/AIDS found in homosexual men. Studies showed that gay or homosexual men were more likely to be infected with the deadly virus as they kept their sexual identities under wraps. A report says that we are 18 times more likely to get HIV from unprotected anal sex than from unprotected vaginal sex.

In July 2018, Justice Chandrachud added, 'Same-sex couples living in denial with no access to medical care were more prone to contracting and spreading sexually-transmitted diseases.'

One of the biggest things I noticed during the final hearing on Section 377 in the Supreme Court was the number of religious bodies standing against reading down of Section 377 despite worshipping in the same temples where images of homosexuality are exalted on the walls. I remember, at the time, every drawing room was full of the same discussion, some in support of same-sex relationships and some against. Strangely, the idea that same-sex relationships should not be allowed was primarily based on remote ideas of religion and *sanskriti,* even though overwhelming evidence exists that our sanskriti has, through the ages, not only been tolerant but also understanding of homosexuality, often carving it on temple walls.

More than an academic change, this judgment has brought about significant and fundamental changes in the lives of the LGBTQIA+ community. The judgment, given by five judges, elaborated on what dignity and individual freedom meant:

> The overarching ideals of individual autonomy and liberty, equality for all sans discrimination of any kind, recognition of identity with dignity and privacy of human beings constitute the cardinal four corners of our monumental Constitution forming the concrete substratum of our fundamental rights that has eluded certain sections of our society who are still living in the bondage of dogmatic social norms, prejudiced notions, rigid stereotypes, parochial mindset and bigoted perceptions. Social exclusion, identity seclusion and isolation from the social mainstream are still the stark realities faced by individuals today and it is only when each and every individual is liberated from the shackles of such bondage and is able to work towards full development of his/her personality that we can call ourselves a truly free society. The first step on the long path to acceptance of the diversity and variegated hues that nature has created has to be taken now by vanquishing the enemies of prejudice and injustice and undoing the wrongs done so as to make way for a progressive and inclusive realisation of social and economic rights embracing all and to begin a dialogue for ensuring equal rights and opportunities for the—less than equall sections of the society. We have to bid adieu to the perceptions, stereotypes and prejudices deeply ingrained in the societal mindset so as to usher in inclusivity in all spheres and empower all citizens alike without any kind of alienation and discrimination.

[...]

> The natural identity of an individual should be treated to be absolutely essential to his being. What nature gives is natural. That is called nature within. Thus, that part of the personality of a person has to be respected and not despised or looked down upon. The said inherent nature and the associated natural impulses in that regard are to be accepted. Non-acceptance of it by any societal norm or notion and punishment by law on some obsolete idea and idealism affects the kernel of the identity of an individual. Destruction of individual identity would tantamount to crushing of intrinsic dignity that cumulatively encapsulates the values of privacy, choice, freedom of speech and other expressions. It can be viewed from another angle. An individual in exercise of his choice may feel that he/she should be left alone but no one, and we mean, no one, should impose solitude on him/her.

The judgment is landmark in that it gives absolute freedom of sexual orientation without any restriction under the umbrella of the Right to Dignity and Right to Privacy. The judgment recognized an individual's autonomy and absolute right over her/his own body without subscribing to what may be called a majoritarian moral viewpoint. The idea of consent and consensual sexual autonomy was crystallized by this judgment, thus institutionalizing the overarching constitutional morality idealized in our constitution. The idea of 'unnatural offences' and 'carnal intercourse against the order of nature' were regarded to be mere majoritarian views on social morality without any reasonable or scientific basis in the modern era, which the court unanimously held could not be imposed on any part of society.

The court unanimously held that the dignity of an individual is an inseparable facet of human personality, which is one of the most cherished aspects of the Right to Life under Article 21 of the Constitution. It is based upon the idea that the individuality of an individual is recognized, accepted and respected; the respect flows from the conception of dignity, which is a fundamental right under Article 21 of the Constitution. This is an essential aspect of the judgment because the individual autonomy of an individual allows them to behave and conduct themselves according to their desires, which includes the right to choose without fear. The court held that dignity of all is a sacrosanct human right, and sans dignity, human life loses its substantial meaning.

Chief Justice Misra and Justice Indu Malhotra opined that a person's sexual orientation itself is as natural a phenomenon as any other natural phenomenon. The view that the sexual orientation of a person is a natural phenomenon is well based on the concept of individualistic autonomy and the person's natural right to choose the way they want to conduct their personal intimate relations and conduct. The court highlighted that the Constitution aims to transform the society and not entrench and preserve the pre-existing values of the majority.

Section 377 does not consider the presence of 'willful and informed consent,' thereby leading to the criminalization of consensual acts within the LGBTQIA+ community. After 2013, when Section 375 was amended to include anal and certain other kinds of sexual intercourse between a man and a woman that would not be criminalized as rape if it was between consenting adults, it was clear that if Section 377 continues to penalize such sexual intercourse, there lies a contradiction and dichotomy in the law. The striking down of Section 377 puts an end to such a dichotomy in law so that no one provision of the IPC is used according to the whims and fancies of the system to stigmatize a minority.

The court only partially struck down Section 377 as far as it applies to consenting adults. Therefore, an implication here can be drawn that the provision still applies to even consensual sexual intercourse between minors of the same gender.

The concept of individualistic autonomy in itself comprises various fundamental protections granted by the Constitution of India, such as the right to decide how the person should take their decisions, the right of social orientation, etc. The court, in its liberal approach, gives utmost importance to the consent of individuals and therefore upholds the sovereign right of an individual over their personal decisions, thereby not allowing any interference in the personal life of individuals by the State.

Beyond the contours and technicalities of law, what the judgment brings is relief. In an increasingly homophobic and intolerant world, it creates hope that there is someone to listen to the forgotten and the silent. While driving from my chambers to my office in South Delhi on 6 September 2018, I saw the streets of Delhi in colour. The hallowed Bhagwan Das Road, where the Supreme Court is located, witnessed vast crowds of people dancing and celebrating, reminding me of Holi. It reminded me of the days when I was living in New York and had decided to see the Gay Pride Parade on Christopher Street. It was a riot of colour, and the celebration was infectious.

The effect of the judgment is apparent now, years after, the idea of having same-sex couples has suddenly become more acceptable. Today, being a same-sex couple does raise a few eyebrows, but maybe not violence. The change is palpable. Women and men are suddenly free to love who they want to despite their gender. The idea of homosexuality is not a question mark anymore. We have started a march towards acceptance.

A Constitution-Bench of the Hon'ble Supreme Court of India in *Supriyo v. Union of India* was petitioned to interpret the Special

Marriage Act so as to legally recognize marriage between persons of the same sex. The case was passionately argued by India's foremost counsels, many of whom were part of the LGBTQIA+ community. The question of whether the Hon'ble Court in lieu of the string of judgments in Naz Foundation, Navtej Johar and others would legally recognize these Unions as the natural next step gripped the social and academic discourse of our nation. The Hon'ble Court however, ended up in a 3–2 verdict refusing to recognize such a right to enter into a Union deeming it as an exercise beyond their jurisdiction and one for which the legislature is best suited for. This was reasoned as marriage as a socio-legal relationship includes a plethora of other laws that need to be reconciled with this modern understanding of atypical marriages, this included *inter alia* reconciling gendered laws on divorce, alimony, succession, rape and other penal provisions. The Chief Justice D.Y. Chandrachud dispelled the notion that marriage is limited to an exercise of procreation, or somehow the belief that LGBTQIA+ is an urban phenomenon. The Chief Justice engaged with scientific research that reflected that sexuality is something a person is born with and to deprive them of a right to enter a Union would gravely harm the persons personal liberty and freedom of conscience under Article 25. Freedom of conscience is no longer seen merely from the perspective of practicing a religion but includes within this right; the right to make moral choices, to believe what actions are conscionable within the reasonable restriction's classification. The Hon'ble Court granted the rights of heterosexual transgender persons to marry, and within that, recognized transgender persons as including biologically transgender and those who are genderqueer without biological markings. The Hon'ble Court whilst issuing directions of protection from hate crime and discrimination held that a committee with a mandate awarded by Parliament of India would be best suited to undertake legislated endeavours which require stakeholder engagement and a broad and discursive exercise of defining how to constitute the institution of marriage in India. It is a common saying amongst the legal fraternity that a hard-hitting dissent today will shape the constitutional discourse of tomorrow.

I hope and wish that the judgment paves the way for a world where love, in all its multifarious manifestations, is accepted. At this juncture, I do realize that after years of being a taboo, a judgment won't immediately result in the complete and absolute acceptance of LGBTQIA+ identities. Still, perhaps, it serves as a ray of hope. The idea has taken root and will one day bloom into a free world where emotions are recognized for what they are, devoid of any tether to societal gender expectations.

The Right to Die

Aruna Shanbaug

When I was writing this, the whole world was in the grip of a pandemic. A virus, unable to be seen by the naked eye, had taken control of the world as we know it and had upended our entire existence.

The strangest thing about the whole situation was that the whole human race had decided to stay inside to survive. Life is that precious to us. Preservation of life had taken precedence over everything else. Businesses had shut offices, curfew was imposed in cities and life had come to a standstill. Economically, it has been devastating. And still, we are trying to survive.

Growing up, we learnt, whether as a social value, or a moral or religious teaching, whatever you may term it, that life is precious and every anchor of life must strive to safeguard it. The ideology I grew up with is that any man who endangers life or creates obstructions towards life is a wrongdoer and must be punished. As a child growing up with that mindset, it was difficult to grapple with the idea that death might be better than life.

Our Constitution gives us the Right to Life. Over the years, it has included in that ambit a variety of interpretations, like the Right to Clean Air and Water, Right to a Livelihood, Right to Dignity and, most recently, the Right to Die. with the more often used and weaponized is the provision for penalizing the abetment to suicide. Today, I realize how important life is, and how necessary it is to allow us to live it in a way that has the dignity of the right to die. I've come to the conclusion that we as human beings, barring some extraordinary circumstances, put in our best efforts to preserve our lives, so when we ask to let go of it, it is not a decision to be taken lightly.

In India, the idea of euthanasia is synonymous with the horrifying story of Aruna Shanbaug, the nurse at KEM Hospital in the sprawling metropolis of Mumbai. Aruna's life was the synonym of a bright future—young and vibrant, she was a nurse at the hospital and engaged to be married to a doctor who loved her. It was a life singing with hope.

WHAT HAPPENED TO ARUNA?

It was the morning of 27 November 1973 that turned the young nurse's life on its head, and ignited questions in India that finally culminated in 2018. What is life? What are the components of life? Who is dead and who isn't? Is just breathing enough?

Aruna Shanbaug had woken up with a slight temperature that day, and her niece Mangala Naik had asked her to take leave from the hospital and rest. But Shanbaug, the diligent nurse, said that she needed to see to some work. The next day, her sister got a call from the hospital that Shanbaug had been attacked at King Edward Memorial Hospital, Lower Parel, where she worked as a junior nurse. It was a month before her wedding.

She was in charge of the laboratory where they kept dogs. It was the same department where her attacker, Sohanlal Bhartha Walmiki, worked as a sweeper. Aruna had reported against him for not doing his job properly, and his response was something the whole country would not be able to forget even over half a decade later. He choked her with a dog leash in the basement of the cardiovascular thoracic building and sexually assaulted the young bride to be. She never regained consciousness. Sohanlal was released in 1980 and now reportedly lives in a village in Uttar Pradesh working as a labourer.

The existence of a person in any country is determined by the virtue of being alive. We have the Right to Life. This right, in all its dynamic interpretations, is enshrined in our Constitution, and envelops and protects a person from the moment of birth till the last breath. Right to Life means that a human being has an essential right to live a life of dignity.

Vested with Right to Life, it is only natural to question: do we have the choice to demand euthanasia or mercy killing? Euthanasia is the deliberate termination of a human life when the life of a patient with terminal illness only worsens with time and eventually becomes so unbearable that the patient chooses to die rather than to endure the suffering any longer.

CAN DEATH BE A CHOICE?

It is in these cultural and social circumstances that India examined the Right to Life and the question of whether it also contained the Right to Die With Dignity. What is the correct thing to do when a patient is in irreversible and unmanageable pain, or is for all intents and purposes not living, though only existing by the tenuous thread of breath? The essential question that arises here is whether to wait for a miraculous recovery of the patient and until then to let them continue to endure the suffering, or to let a person end their pain and suffering when there is no hope left.

According to the House of Lords' Select Committee on Medical Ethics, euthanasia is 'a deliberate intervention undertaken with the intention of ending life to relieve intractable suffering'. Thus, it can be said that euthanasia is the deliberate and intentional killing of a human being by a direct action, such as lethal injection, or by the failure to perform even the most basic medical care, or by withdrawing life support system in order to release that human being from a painful life. It is a practice that can ensure that a person lives as well as dies with dignity.

Here exists a conflict of interest, a conflict between the interests of society and that of an individual, which begs the question: which would gain supremacy over the other and emerge as the winner that would ultimately determine the continued life and existence of a person?

There has been no consensus on the issue in *Maruti Shripati Dubal v. State of Maharastra,* where a police constable, who had developed schizophrenia due to injuries, had tried to die by suicide. The Bombay High Court held that Right to Life under Article 21 of the Constitution of India includes the Right to Die. While in the case of *Chenna Jagadeeswar v. State of AP*, where a doctor was charged with killing his four children and attempt to die by suicide, the Andhra Pradesh High Court said that the Right to Die is not a fundamental right under Article 21 of the Constitution. In P. Rathinam's case, the Supreme Court of India observed that the Right to Life includes the Right to Die, or to terminate one's life, and then again in *Gain Kaur v. State of Punjab*, a five-member bench overruled the P. Rathainam's case and held that Right to Life under Article 21 does not include right to die or the Right to Die.

A landmark judgment passed by Justice Markandey Katju and Justice Gyan Sudha Misra tends to legalize passive euthanasia. The case was filed for grant of permission by one writer and social activist Pinky Virani on behalf of Aruna Ramachandra Shanbaug, who, by that time, had been in a persistent vegetative state for 37 years at Mumbai's KEM Hospital. During Aruna's case, the judges commented on deletion of Section 309 of the IPC, as it had become anachronistic. It was held in Aruna's case that in case the patient is incompetent in deciding whether their life support system should be discontinued, family members or close relatives, or in their absence, doctors attending to the patient, can decide in the best interests of the patient with the bona fide intention. However, such a decision requires approval from the concerned High Court.

Euthanasia is categorized into two types: active euthanasia or assisted suicide, where the patient (usually terminally ill or in intractable pain) asks the doctors to give them lethal medication, mostly either oral or intravenously; and passive euthanasia, where life support systems are withdrawn, and the person is allowed to pass on without resuscitation or giving any forced life-preserving treatments.

To understand the varied aspects of euthanasia, it is imperative to draw out a distinction between euthanasia and suicide. It is not the same and there exists a conceptual distinction. Suicide, as mentioned in the Oxford Dictionary, means the act of killing yourself deliberately. The Bombay High Court in Maruti Shripati Dubal Case has attempted to make a distinction between suicide and euthanasia or mercy killing. The court held that suicide, by its very nature, is an act of self-killing or termination of one's own life by one's act without assistance from others, and euthanasia means the intervention of other human agency to end life. Mercy killing, therefore, cannot be considered on the same footing as suicide. Mercy killing is homicide, whatever the circumstance in which it is committed. The two concepts are both factually and legally distinct.

Coming to the legal aspect of euthanasia in India, it has to be acknowledged that it cannot and should not be studied in isolation. In India, euthanasia is undoubtedly illegal. Since in cases of euthanasia or mercy killing there is an intention on the part of the doctor to kill the patient, such cases would clearly fall under Clause 1 of Section 300 of the IPC, 1860. However, in such cases where there is valid consent of the deceased, Exception 5 to the said Section would be attracted and the doctor or mercy killer would be punishable under Section 304 for culpable homicide not amounting to murder. But it is only cases of voluntary euthanasia (where the patient consents to death) that would attract Exception 5 to Section 300. Cases of non-voluntary and involuntary euthanasia would be struck by proviso one to Section 92 of the IPC and thus be rendered illegal. The law in India is also very clear on the aspect of assisted suicide. Right to suicide is not an available 'right' in India — it is punishable under the IPC. Provision of punishing suicide is contained in Sections 305 (Abetment of Suicide of Child or Insane Person), 306 (Abetment of Suicide) and 309 (Attempt to Commit Suicide) of the said code. Section 309, IPC, has been brought under the scanner with regards to its constitutionality as the Right to Life is an important right enshrined in Constitution of India. It is argued that the Right to Life under Article 21 also includes the Right to Die. Therefore, mercy killing is a legal right of a person.

The judgment of the Supreme Court in *Aruna Ramchandra Shanbaug v. Union of India* opened the gateway for the legalization of passive euthanasia. A petition was filed before the Supreme Court for seeking permission for euthanasia for one Aruna Ramchandra Shanbaug as she was in a persistent vegetative state (PVS) and in essence not alive, had no awareness and was brain dead for all intents and purposes. The Supreme Court established a committee for medical examination of the patient to ascertain the issue, eventually dismissing the petition, observing that although passive euthanasia is permissible under supervision of law in exceptional circumstances, active euthanasia is not permitted under the law.

The court laid down the guidelines, which will continue to be until the Parliament intervenes:

1. A decision has to be taken to discontinue life support either by the parents or the spouse or other close relatives, or in the absence of any of them. Such a decision can be taken even by a person or a body of persons acting as a next friend. It can also be taken by the doctors attending the patient. However, the decision should be taken bona fide in the best interest of the patient.
2. Hence, even if a decision is taken by the near relatives or doctors or next friend to withdraw life support, such a decision requires approval from the High Court concerned.

Aruna Shanbaug passed away in 2016 of natural causes, after a battle of decades. The reports have indicated that the nurses of KEM hospital, where she worked and lived for the majority of her life, made her life as comfortable as possible, saluting the brave woman in the end with flowers and giving her a send-off befitting a queen. Aruna Shanbaug was one case, the one highlighted and the one we know about, but what about other cases of people who are suffering a similar fate or worse?

The Supreme Court in 2018, in a landmark change in law and attitude, has allowed passive euthanasia and forged a way for the creation of a living will. Holding that Right to Die with Dignity is a fundamental right, the bench has held that passive euthanasia and a living will is legally valid, giving detailed guidelines. The bench comprising of Chief Justice Dipak Misra and Justices A.K. Sikri, A.M. Khanwilkar, D.Y. Chandrachud and Ashok Bhushan delivered the verdict on a PIL filed by the NGO Common Cause.

The petition was filed for seeking a system for certification and for legally recognizing a 'living will'.

The petition raised the question: how can a person be told that s/he does not have right to prevent torture on his body? Right to Life includes Right to Die with Dignity. A person cannot be forced to live on support of ventilator. Keeping a patient alive by artificial means against his/her wishes is an assault on his/her body.

The bench, while passing this landmark judgment, held that the right to live with dignity also includes the smoothening of the process of dying in case of a terminally ill patient or a person in PVS with no hope of recovery. The Chief Justice said:

> A failure to legally recognize advance medical directives may amount to non-facilitation of the right to smoothen the dying process and the right to live with dignity. Further, a study of the position in other jurisdictions shows that Advance Directives have gained lawful recognition in several jurisdictions by way of legislation and in certain countries through judicial pronouncements. Though the sanctity of life has to be kept on the high pedestal yet in cases of terminally ill persons or PVS patients where there is no hope for revival, priority shall be given to the Advance Directive and the right of self-determination. In the absence of Advance Directive, the procedure provided for the said category hereinbefore shall be applicable. When passive euthanasia as a situational palliative measure becomes applicable, the best interest of the patient shall override the State interest. […] The Right to Life and liberty as envisaged under Article 21 of the Constitution is meaningless unless it encompasses within its sphere individual dignity. With the passage of time, this Court has expanded the spectrum of Article 21 to include

> within it the right to live with dignity as component of Right to Life and liberty.

Further, Justice D.Y. Chandrachud very rightly concluded: 'The right of an individual to refuse medical treatment is unconditional. Neither the law nor the constitution can compel an individual who is competent and able to take decisions to disclose reasons for refusing medical treatment nor is such a refusal subject to the supervisory control of an outside entity.'

In a unanimous judgment, the Supreme Court accorded primacy to the constitutional values of liberty, dignity, autonomy and privacy as it laid down procedural guidelines governing the advance directive of a living will. The guidelines will operate till legislation is put in place. While debating the legalization of euthanasia, sanctity of life notwithstanding, the opposition to euthanasia breeds from the fear of misuse of the right if it is permitted.

It is feared that placing the discretion in the hands of the doctor would be placing too much power in his hands and he may misuse such power. This fear stems largely from the fact that the discretionary power is placed in the hands of non-judicial personnel (a doctor in this case). This is so because we do not shirk from placing the same kind of power in the hands of a judge (for example, when we give the judge the power to decide whether to award a death sentence or a sentence of imprisonment for life). But what is surprising is that the fear is of the very person (the doctor) in whose hands we would otherwise not be afraid of placing our lives. A doctor with a scalpel in his hands is acceptable but not a doctor with a fatal injection.

What is even more surprising is that ordinarily the law does not readily accept negligence on the part of a doctor. The courts tread with great caution when examining the decision of a doctor and yet his decision in cases of euthanasia is not considered reliable. It is felt that a terminally ill patient who suffers from unbearable pain should be allowed to die. Indeed, spending valuable time, money and facilities on a person who has neither the desire nor the hope of recovery is nothing but a waste of the same. At this juncture, it would not be out of place to mention that the 'liberty to die', if not right in strict sense, may be read as part of the Right to Life guaranteed by Article 21 of the Constitution of India.

The debate escalates while determining the legalization of voluntary (both active and passive) euthanasia. This is because, though there may be some cases of non-voluntary or involuntary euthanasia where one may sympathize with the patient and in which one may agree that letting the patient die was the best possible option, it is believed that it would be very difficult to separate each case from other cases of non-voluntary or involuntary euthanasia. Thus, it is believed that the potential of misuse of provisions allowing non-voluntary and involuntary euthanasia is far greater than that of the misuse of provisions seeking to permit voluntary euthanasia.

Another fascinating aspect that gets involved here is the way medical professionals deal with the issue. For most, that I came across, as long as there was a registered living will with a 'do not resuscitate' (DNR) clause, there didn't seem to be an issue. However, when it came to the issue of children or family members taking the call to ease the suffering of their elder, the threat of a court proceeding or an allegation of misuse is enough to keep the doctors and the family members away from signing the papers for removal of life-supporting equipment. The issue is more than a legalistic matter; it is an issue that involves some of the most basic human emotions—letting go of a loved one. Beyond the cut and dry problems of court cases and allegations of misuse, at the very end, it is about giving our loved ones a dignity in death.

As of today, a living will seems to be the most plausible way, as it records the intention of one still alive and cogent patient, to be allowed dignity in death, if they desired it to be so. There are risks, no doubt, and there is an urgent and a palpable need for judicial as well as civil discipline. It is an emerging issue that has just gotten the right impetus. With time and further adjudication, this will soon be an embodiment of our core constitutional as well as human principles.

Wayward Sons

Repatriating ISIS

The world seems to have changed in many ways. When I was growing up, times were simpler. There were no cellphones or constant access to the Internet, and the world seemed to be a smaller place, confined only to the *mohalla* we lived in or perhaps the city. The biggest international problems that we used to face as citizens were taxes and foreign policy, simply because we did not know what lay beyond our borders. Times were so simple that we only knew what was printed, and the constant noise of 24-hour news did not exist. Although today we marvel at the age of technology, but we often ignore the downsides of it. Sometimes it is because we are not faced with them directly, and other times because the influx of information is almost overwhelming and has desensitized us to violence.

There is, I believe, a sense of urgency that prevails in the world we inhabit today, as opposed to what our elders felt when they were my age. The youth today is definitely the future, as it has always been. However, the difference is that the youth today also have, at their fingertips, immense power in the form of the Internet, and sometimes it is this very power that leads the youth astray.

In our country, radicalization is a relatively new term. It is not that we have had a completely homogenous culture, but it has never been as oil and water as it is today. Our school textbooks have called us a 'nation of diversity' and for most part of our history, it has been true. We are a nation of diversity, and like every culture, we have our own peculiarities and religious heterogeneity.

When the 9/11 attacks happened on the Twin Towers in the US, the world watched with horror. I remember someone called me to switch on the television, and we all watched the first tower collapsing, and then another plane came and hit the second tower. At that time, there was no way we could have predicted the impact it would have on world politics. It seemed like overnight the world had woken up to Islamic terrorism, and the impact it could have. Things that had seemed so far away from us had suddenly become possible terrors. It was the incident that started the idea of 'terror attacks', something that we still grapple with.

Al-Qaeda was then heralded as the face of Islamic terrorism in all countries. Osama bin Laden was the face of Al-Qaeda and the largest manhunt in the history of the world was launched, finally culminating in 2011, in the small town of Abottabad in Pakistan. Al-Qaeda spawned a multitude of organizations, one of which rose to become the most dreaded, now called ISIS.

The Islamic State has several names—ISIS, Daesh and ISIL. It emerged from the Iraqi faction of the Al-Qaeda founded by Abu Musab al-Zarqawi in 2004. The organization did not gain much traction in its initial years, almost fading into obscurity till the Iraqi revolution. The fall of Saddam Hussein, and his subsequent imprisonment and execution on 30 December 2006 pushed the organization further into the background. After the fall of Osama bin Laden and the fragmentation of the Al-Qaeda, Daesh, following a Salafist jihadism ideology, began re-emerging from its hideout to take advantage of the instability in the region of Syria and Iraq.

Over and over they changed form, finally renaming

themselves the 'Islamic State of Iraq and Syria' in 2013, launching its offensive operations in the cities of Tikrit and Mosul. It was then that the leader Abu Bakr al-Baghdadi from inside The Great Mosque of al-Nuri in Iraq's second-largest city of Mosul, changed the name again to 'Islamic State', clearly signalling the intention of going beyond the borders of Iraq and Syria and announced the formation of an Islamic caliphate from Diyala in Northern and Western Iraq to Aleppo in Eastern Syria, thus starting its reign of terror.

The fortunes of ISIS have, over the years, risen and fallen, as the politics of the region became more and more volatile. Even while President Donald Trump declared the defeat of the Islamic State, my concern is a little closer to home. In the caliphate's five years, thousands of recruits from various countries across the world—including Saudi Arabia, France, Australia and Tunisia—have made their way to Iraq and Syria; and a forgotten name in this list is India.

The nature of India's diversity makes it unique, as does its connection to the Asiatic landmass. Afghanistan is a near neighbour as there are routes through Pakistan. With a large population of Muslims, our youth becomes prime targets for radicalization and induction as fighters. The state of Kerala seems most affected by this phenomenon.

With the strengths of technology, come its weakness and temptations too. In this case, it is online propaganda designed to lure young Muslims into a fantastical and misguided ideology, asking them to fight a war for the sake of religion. 'Jihad' or the 'holy war' which is almost magnetic. The idea that we can create a difference, or that we may be useful to our communities in some way are almost ingrained in the human species. But when it takes the wrong turn, it creates a situation where we become pawns of powers we do not quite fully realize. In July 2020, the National

Investigation Agency (NIA) filed a chargesheet referencing the module Al-Hind, where the Islamic State has been plotting to create a province in the jungles of Aouth India.

I think it was around April 2017 when I first heard about the 'mother of all bombs'. The USA dropped a GBU-43/B Massive Ordnance Air Blast in Afghanistan's Nangarhar province, a remote mountainous region, to target the ISKP. It was then that some youths from Kerala were caught. There were also reports of young Indians having been killed in the fighting in Afghanistan.

The malaise seems to be affected through citizens returning from the Middle East, a region with which it has deep ties. A report on the Internet regarding Abdul Rashid Abdullah describes him as a preacher. He has been reportedly accused of radicalizing students in Kerala and encouraging them to join the Islamic State in Afghanistan. Reported to be an educated man, Adbul Rashid Abdullah was reportedly an engineer who left his job in the private sector and took to teaching hardened radicalized interpretations of Islam after the unfortunate death of his first born. It was then that he started teaching the Quran aligned with how the Islamic State interprets the holy scripture. The idea that he allegedly taught to gather foot warriors for the Islamic State was that it is impossible to wage jihad from inside the country and that the only way for the holy religion to reach the subcontinent is to support ISIS efforts in Afghanistan, which would then lead them to conquer India, making it an extension of the declared caliphate.

Another fast-growing aspect of this is the continuous misinformation and the untrue rhetoric of Muslim marginalization that has spread. It has contributed to the Indian Muslim being vulnerable to predators like these, who draft Indians and then smuggle them outside the borders to function as fighters.

The question of how citizens are indoctrinated is a multifold one, however, the issue that concerns me the most is what happens to these people once they leave Indian borders—whether they can return to their families when they are disillusioned, or whether it is a fate that they have subjected themselves to, for the rest of their lives.

THE ISIS BRIDES CASES

It was a newspaper report that first alerted me to the extent of this problem. In March 2020, a prominent newspaper reported on a story of Nimisha, alias Fathima Isa, a resident of Thiruvananthapuram, who had left India in the company of 21 other operatives to join the Islamic State in Afghanistan in 2016.[1] In 2020, she was 31 years old and was reportedly a mother to a baby girl. The report said that she was seeking the government's help to return to India. *The Week* ran a story detailing the lives and the wait of three women in Kerala, whose children had left to join ISIS.[2]

The emotional article detailed the life of Bindu Sampath, a 50-year-old woman, whose daughter Nimisha was studying in a dental college. After Nimisha, or Fatima as she is now known, went missing, Bindu seemed to blame herself for whatever had happened. She laments that she should have been more accepting of her daughter, her conversion from Hinduism to Islam, and should have kept a more watchful eye.

She said that the last time she saw Nimisha and her husband

---

[1]KP, Saikiran, 'Situation in Caliphate Disappointing: Malayali ISIS Women in Afghanistan Want to Return', *The Times of India*, 17 March 2020, https://tinyurl.com/yxuxn2de. Accessed on 27 November 2023.

[2]Nayar, Mandira, 'Long Legal Battle Awaits Four Kerala Women Who Joined ISIS', *The Week*, 12 June 2021, https://tinyurl.com/d79k9ypx. Accessed on 27 November 2023.

Bexon, another convert, was in 2016, when her child was seven months pregnant. They stayed with her for a day and told her that they were going to Sri Lanka. She says that since then, all contact she's had with them was when they had messaged her on Telegram that they had reached Syria.

Nimisha's husband Bexon and his brother Bestin are also among the group that went as fighters to the ISIS. The mothers of both the boys and the girl are now in constant touch and praying for the well-being of their children. Bindu has not heard from her daughter ever since she and her husband left India, but did come to know through Bexon's mother that the two had a daughter. Then, she is still awaiting the return of her daughter. Nimisha was in prision till August 2021, till the Taliban gained control of Afghanistan. She was released from prison. Nimisha's girl child is at present around 5 years of age and the distraught grandmother has approached the Central Government to rescue the child from the hands of the ruthless Taliban Government.

Bexon and Bestin's mother Gracey also lives in Kerala. Her sons were raised in a Christian household and she says that they were religious from the beginning, never missing Mass. She says she started sensing a change in their behaviour when her own marital problems started and their father started living with another woman. She believes that a person named M.M. Akbar had a significant role to play in the conversion and radicalization of both her sons. Akbar was later nabbed by the police for promoting communal enmity through objectionable content in textbooks.

The story of Merrin was as different from the two boys as it could be. She came from an upper-caste Brahmin family and was considered the smartest of the lot. Gracey says that she remembers Merrin as vivacious and cheerful. She was in the same class as the other three and they became friends. She started dating Bestin, who was by then already on the path to conversion, but they ended their relationship when she left to work in Mumbai. Bestin followed her to Mumbai and then supposedly impressed the ideas that he was so taken in by on her, and she converted to Islam and followed him to Khorasan. There are rumours that she has now married Abdul Rasheed, after Bestin passed away while fighting.

Merrin, or Mariyam as she is called after converting, was interviewed by a journalist about her journey in an Afghan prison, after the fall of ISIS in 2019. She was imprisoned in a dimly lit cell with both her children, one aged three and another around 10 months at the time. Twice widowed by then, she had been held along with seven other women by Afghanistan's spy agency, the National Directorate of Security, after the Afghan National Forces retook Nangarhar from ISIS in November 2020.

Now, as the Islamic State has fallen, the problem for India becomes bigger. The fighters, their wives and families are disillusioned with the promises that were made to them, and they now want to return to their homeland.

In 2020, Strat News Global uploaded a video detailed the journey of the 21 men and women who'd travelled from India to Afghanistan.[3] One of the women was the wife of the handler Abdul Rashid Abdullah, who had arranged this journey and had been allegedly spreading Islamic State propaganda in Kerala. They reportedly crossed over to Afghanistan on foot from Iran. Abdullah, who hails from Pala in Kerala, had been reportedly the main conspirator for Islamic State recruitment in Kerala. His wife Sonia Sebastian alias Ayisha was one of the women who has

---

[3]Revi, Amitabh P., 'Khorasan Files:The Journey of Indian 'Islamic State' Widows', *Strat News Global*, 10 June 2020, https://tinyurl.com/yc373ph5. Accessed on 20 November 2023.

appealed for the government's help to return to India. She can be heard saying, 'I came to Khorasan in 2016. Once we reached here, many things we saw were not up to our expectations. We expected to live an Islamic life under Islamic law. That is not what the reality is. Now, I want to return to India to my husband's family.'

On 11 November 2019, a court in The Hague ruled that the Netherlands must actively help repatriate the children of women who joined Islamic State, and who are currently being held in prison camps in Syria. Lawyers for the 23 women who had joined ISIS had previously argued for the court to force (obligation of result) the State to repatriate them and their 56 children. However, the final ruling stopped short of such an obligation and instead compelled the State to merely do everything within reasonable limits to repatriate the children (obligation of effort).

The State immediately announced that it would appeal the ruling. It argued that the court had failed to take into account national security interests and diplomatic considerations. On 22 November, the court of Appeal overturned the previous decision and ruled that the State was, in fact, not legally required to assist in the repatriation of the children.

After the initial ruling, social media was awash with outcries of both horror and joy. The subject of repatriation and prosecution of foreign fighters proved to be an incredibly divisive issue. Complex questions arose. Is the State responsible for its own war criminals? Does the State have the duty of care in these cases? Do foreign fighters still have a right to citizenship? Increasingly, the legal debate has been muddled by moral considerations and cries for modification of the legal framework in order to deal with the issues at hand. The legal disagreements as well as the moral contention and emotional outcry surrounding the issue illustrate the complexity of the problem of returning foreign fighters.

The leading consideration with regard to the question of

repatriation is the potential threat that returning foreign fighters might pose to national security, which strongly divides expert opinion. On one end of the spectrum, there are those that argue that it is safer to have the fighters prosecuted and in prison, so that they can be monitored and possibly deradicalized. This line of argument proposes that leaving violent extremists to roam the Middle East and beyond, ultimately poses a bigger threat, since there is no way of controlling or monitoring them.

Opponents of this theory claim that in view of the training and experience these fighters have gained while in Syria, it is, in fact, a bigger threat to have them within our own borders. They argue that the Dutch justice system is not equipped for this new type of criminal and the complexity of their offences. This inadequacy means that if convicted, these fighters would serve sentences with an average of six years, after which they would be released into society. Indeed, recent sentences passed in 'terrorism trials' are mild compared to those passed in other European countries. These milder sentences are a direct result of the legal quagmire that these trials present.

One of the biggest prosecutorial headaches in these cases is the burden of proof. Evidentiary challenges mean that in many cases the public prosecution can only prove that individuals were present in enemy territory, not that they were members of a terrorist organization, or prove their active participation in violent crimes. Only if there is evidence of membership of a terrorist organization, or evidence of war crimes can additional charges be brought and higher sentences be passed.

A second complicating factor is the legal base for convictions and the absence of any specific legal framework for terrorist crimes. While regular criminal law provisions might be sufficient to secure a conviction in some cases, punishments may be light, not reflecting the full severity of the case. However, while the Dutch system relies on its ordinary criminal code, it does provide for the added charge of 'terrorist intent', which enables prosecutors to add legal 'weight' to the crime without having to prove a completely separate offence.

Beyond the legal complexities of prosecution, the question of what to do with foreign fighters has put some of our core values up for debate. While the Netherlands does not support capital punishment and has signed the International Convention on Human Rights, several politicians have argued in favour of letting the captured Dutch fighters be tried in Iraq or Syria, where they would likely be put to death. In that context, the death penalty has been called the 'ultimate consequence'. The fate of the children of captured foreign fighters is an even more sensitive issue. While most agree that these children cannot be held accountable for their parents' crimes, the question of whether this means that the State has the moral obligation to try to repatriate them has been an ongoing matter of contention.

The current response to the threat of returning foreign fighters in the Netherlands can be characterized as a combination of preparation and denial. On the one hand, the Dutch State has started preparing for the potential return of foreign fighters, more or less since the first ones started to leave the country. The public prosecution service has made extensive preparations for criminal investigation and prosecution of those fighters, in case they return home. On the other hand, the current political attitude reflects a level of denial of responsibility for the return of these fighters and their civil rights. While it looks like the government is off the hook for now, the debate around their return is unlikely to go away anytime soon.

Similar questions have been raised in India about Areeb Ejaz Majeed, a young boy whose bail was upheld by the Bombay High Court in February 2021 citing the right to a speedy trial. There seems to be conflicting stands on how he was recovered. The NIA claims that he was apprehended while trying to sneak back into the country to carry out terrorist act, while Majeed claims that he was brought back to the country with the help of the NIA, after spending six months in Baghdad. The allegations of him being a part of ISIS have been dropped. In his bail plea, Majeed said that as a 21-year-old, he was 'carried away' and had committed a serious mistake for which he had already spent over six years behind bars. He denied that he had participated in any terrorist activity in Iraq or planned to commit one after his return to India.

Majeed, a resident of Kalyan, had been a civil engineering student in 2014 when he along with three others, namely Aman Tandel, Fahad Shaikh and Saheen Tanki, boarded an Etihad Airways flight for Abu Dhabi and travelled to Baghdad with a group of pilgrims. The four youths later separated from the group, went to Syria and joined the Islamic State, said investigating agencies. Their family members filed missing complaints and the NIA later took over the probe.

In August 2014, Majeed's family said that they had received a phone call from Tanki, who reportedly told them that Majeed had died. But three months later, on 29 November 2014, Majeed was arrested at the Mumbai airport.

He has been in jail since then, charged with offences under Section 16 and Section 18 of the Unlawful Activities (Prevention) Act, read with Section 125 (waging war against any Asiatic power in alliance with the Government of India) under the IPC, which has a maximum punishment of life imprisonment. He was also charged with being a member of a terrorist organization, but the Special Court dropped this charge in 2017.

Since that Islamic State is an organization that has been banned in India, members who have been a part of it or involved in it are subject to incarceration under our IPC. There is no stopping the prosecution or an option for waiver of the charges. The fall of ISIS and the takeover of Afghanistan by the Taliban has further complicated the matters.

The Internet seems to be full of appeals of the families of these fighters, cajoling and begging the government to allow these women and men to return, but to what extent can we allow that? Even as a mother myself, I cannot pretend to imagine the immeasurable pain that these women have undergone and are in even today. On the other hand, it is a very real fear for me that allowing these children to return might cause more mothers to lose their children.

Private/Public

Aadhaar and The Right to Privacy

'To be left alone is the most precious thing one can ask of the modern world.'

—Anthony Burgess, English writer and composer

We live in a world that is vastly different from what it was 30 years ago. And as is the nature of things, these differences are often attributed to the colloquial 'generation gap'. Societies have changed drastically and fundamentally, and needs, requirements and thought processes have changed too. To me, it feels like the current generation has so exponentially outpaced the previous ones that the differences span several generational gaps. One could almost call it a 'generational chasm'. I say that because the considerations of the youth today are very different from when I was young. When we were young, we were worried about tangible problems like a thief sneaking into our homes and stealing the newly acquired television set or raiding the traditional *tijori*. Money kept in the bank was the gold standard of safety, and the idea of identity theft was limited to someone saying they knew someone.

Those were simpler times. When the Internet reached India in the early '90s, our idea of the Internet was connectivity, discovering chat rooms, information that could be transferred in the blink of an eye, our work, documents and research. It has largely been a boon, but as with everything, there are some serious downsides as well. They say every invention, after a little while, takes a life of its own, and the Internet is no exception. Today, we have everything available at the click of a button. My juniors order their groceries online and pay online, my daughter orders her clothes and essentials online, one can get their identity documents processed online.

While we put everything we own, think and see online through web portals, we are acutely aware, that now, unlike before, we are not the only ones who have access to these documents. It's not just two or three people who have access to who I am—my records, my place of birth, my social security documents or my life insurance policies. My identity is subject to being hacked and stolen, in much worse ways.

Identity theft is a complicated issue for my generation. We are not used to the idea of having our identities being capable of being stolen, because for most of our lives, they were not virtual entities but tangible documents we could carry and store. We never really gave it a serious thought, or understood the ramifications of it beyond mere academic interest, until the issue over the Aadhaar Act cropped up with furore.

To understand the concern that surround Aadhaar, we first need to understand that India lives in two states simultaneously, and that the Government of India has the unenviable responsibility of saddling the fine line between the two. The India that we as the urban populace know and understand is very different from the India of nearly 60 per cent of the country that is rural. The readers, who may be reading this as an e-book, ordered from their smartphones or computers, paid for by a bank transfer through a computer or a smartphone; and me, writing this draft on my latest acquisition from the Apple Store, while my other gadgets charge nearby, is not the universal experience of the country.

The India we need to address is the India of the 60 per cent. They are the farmers of Vidarbha who probably have no idea what a smartphone is and might not know that a *seb* is called an apple in English. That is the India that needs our help, which successive governments have been trying to do.

During the Covid-19 pandemic, we saw a mass attempt at migration of labour from urban cities to their hometowns. Commendably, our government arranged facilities of medical help and food rations for all those stranded away from their villages. It is in times like these that we see the huge role of Unique Identification Authority of India (UIDAI) in making sure the benefits of the government schemes reached the population that needed it the most. While we worry about identity theft and bank account hacking, there is a population in India that needs welfare and food, which can only be provided through these schemes.

The much-demonized Aadhaar is in its essence an identification that gives the citizen a unique identification number, and it is a database for all personal information from biometrics to address, linking all accounts, bank, phone, broadband, etc. More importantly, Aadhaar is a tool that the government has created to be able to benefit the poor and the needy, who are still reliant on the rains or unpredictable weather, which has been much worsened due to a increasing population and climate disturbances. Aadhaar, contrary to popular belief, is not a tool for a big brother sort of surveillance. Instead, it is a compilation of the last 70 years of failed or partially successful attempts at a delivery mechanism for welfare and benefits where they are most needed.

One of the biggest criticisms of the Aadhaar scheme is with regards to infringement of individual privacy. As a concept, privacy is as old as the human civilization. It encompasses (among other things) freedom of thought, control over one's body, solitude in one's home, control over personal information, freedom from surveillance, protection of one's reputation and protection from searches and interrogations. People in various ages throughout history have understood the concept differently, but never could anyone interpret its true character and meaning. Daniel J. Solove, in his book *Understanding Privacy,* states that 'Privacy is a plurality of different things and that the quest for a singular essence of privacy leads to a dead end.'[1]

The idea of privacy today mostly relates to the digital context, and when we talk of privacy, we are often referring to 'information privacy'. Roger Clarke tried to define 'information privacy' as 'the interest an individual has in controlling, or at least significantly influencing, the handling of data about themselves'.[2]

Today, we all prefer using technology to achieve our desired objectives. For instance, on a daily basis, we make use of technology in transferring money from one person to the other; paying off our phone, electricity, water and food bills; delivering office presentations, sending emails, clicking photographs; and even for socializing with family and friends. Most of this information, then, present on various servers, is left vulnerable to innumerable multinational corporations, private organizations and security agencies who poach personal data belonging to users for profiling and selective advertising of their products.

For instance, Facebook, as we all know, in December 2019 lost personal data consisting of user IDs, phone numbers and names of nearly 49 million Instagram users and 419 million

---

[1]Solove, Daniel J., *Understanding Privacy*, Harvard University Press, 2009, p. ix.

[2]Clarke, Roger, 'Introduction to Dataveillance and Information Privacy, and Definitions of Terms', *Roger Clarke,* 24 July 2016, https://bit.ly/3VIrScj. Accessed on 2 December 2022.

Facebook users in databases online. This information was freely available for access to anyone for almost two weeks, thus leaving users susceptible to SMS spams and phishing attacks.[3]

The idea of privacy in the legislative domain came to be first recognized through the Universal Declaration of Human Rights (UDHR) in 1948. Article 12 of the Universal Declaration of Human Rights of 1948 states that 'No one shall be subjected to arbitrary interference with his privacy, family, home or correspondence, nor to attacks upon his honour and reputation. Everyone has the right to the protection of the law against such interference or attacks'. Similarly, Article 17 of the International Covenant on Civil and Political Rights, 1966, expressed identical terms. Even Article 8 of the European Convention of Human Rights, 1950, concerning 'right to respect for private and family life' states that 'Everyone has the right to respect for his private and family life, his home and his correspondence. There shall be no interference by a public authority with the exercise of this right except such as is in accordance with the law and is necessary in a democratic society in the interests of national security, public safety or the economic well-being of the country, for the prevention of disorder or crime, for the protection of health or morals, or for the protection of the rights and freedoms'.

No express provision of the Constitution of India adumbrates the right to privacy, which means that the existence of such a right becomes determinative from the court's interpretation of the contours of such a right. In real-life terms, it means that the idea of what is privacy and what might constitute infringement of privacy is reliant on how the judiciary decides it is. As society evolves, so does our interpretation—what was not considered

---

[3]Ganjoo, Shweta, 'Facebook faces another data breach, data of 267 million users exposed', 20 December 2019, https://tinyurl.com/5n72czcc. Accessed on 24 November 2023.

private 50 years ago, is today a matter of absolute privacy. When the contours of privacy remain undefined, that would translate to privacy itself being fluid and subject to moral and societal mores. In early cases of *M.P Sharma v. Satish Chandra*, in 1954, where it was held that the provision for a search warrant under CrPC does not offend Article 19 of the Constitution, and in *Kharak Singh v. State of UP*, where this issue came up for consideration, it was held that violation of privacy is not an infringement of any fundamental right guaranteed under Part III of the Constitution. However, it did go on to hold that the right of a person to not to be disturbed at his residence by the State and its officers is recognized to be a part of a fundamental right guaranteed under Article 21 of the Constitution. This was the first time when the recognition of privacy was considered by Indian courts.

Another earlier judgment that lays the foundation of the idea of what privacy was understood to be was *Gobind v. State of MP*, where it was held that privacy is understood to be related to the concept of liberty, which in itself exists via contribution of various fundamental rights. This case later helped in laying the foundation for various decisions asserting the concept. For instance, in *R. Rajagopal v. State of Tamil Nadu*, the court held that the Right to Privacy is implicit under Article 21 of the Constitution of India and similarly in *People's Union for Civil Liberties (PUCL) v. Union of India* the court decided that the Right to Privacy in so far as it pertains to speech is part of the fundamental rights as enshrined under Articles 19(1)(a) and 21 of the Constitution of India.

With several divergent opinions and violations of institutional integrity and judicial discipline, a nine-judge bench of the Supreme Court, through a recent judgment passed in case of *K.S. Puttaswamy v. Union of India* (more commonly known as the Aadhaar case), unanimously decided that the Right to Privacy is a constitutionally protected right, which can be traced through Articles 14, 19 and 21 of the Constitution of India.

It is in the core of Article 21 that the roots to rights to privacy lie. Article 21 enumerates the Right to Life guaranteed to the citizens of India. It is from this Right to Life, that the right to a dignified life emerges, and from here emerges the right to privacy, which is a precondition to the right to a dignified life. The only limitation that Article 21 envisages on this is any invasion of 'Right to Life' or subsequently Right to Privacy has to be done in accordance with and justified on the basis of 'procedure established by law'. An invasion of life and personal liberty and thus of privacy must meet the threefold requirements of: (i) legality, which postulates the existence of law; (ii) need, defined in terms of a legitimate State aim; and (iii) proportionality, which ensures a rational nexus between the objects and the means adopted to achieve them.

The idea of privacy is not just necessary, it is, in fact, the core of the Constitution. Privacy signifies individual dignity and thus the protection of privacy becomes one of the first and foremost duties of the State. Fundamental rights seek to achieve for each individual the dignity of existence. Privacy ensures the fulfilment of dignity and is a value that Article 21 intends to achieve. Dignity cannot exist without privacy. Both reside within the inalienable values of life, liberty and freedom recognized by the Constitution. Dignity of an individual was internationally recognized as an important facet of human rights in 1948 with the enactment of the Universal Declaration of Human Rights. Human dignity not only finds place in our Preamble but also in Article 1 of the same.

Human dignity has been treated as a fundamental right and as a facet not only of Article 21 but that of Right to Equality (Article 14) and also part of bouquet of freedoms stipulated in Article 19.

In *National Legal Service Authority v. Union of India*, the case which was monumental in granting recognition to transgenders, recognition of human dignity was considered to yield happiness to the individuals concerned. Advancement in conceptualizing the doctrine of human dignity took place in *Shabnam v. Union of India*, wherein the court decided to protect certain rights of death convicts by holding that they cannot be executed till they exhaust all available constitutional and statutory remedies. Similarly, in *Jeeja Ghosh v. Union of India*, the court, considering the rights of the disabled and expanding the jurisprudential basis, outlined three important models of dignity—theological, philosophical and constitutional. Lastly, the concept of human dignity based on Right to Autonomy and Right of Choice was explained in detail in *Common Cause v. Union of India*.

The concept of human dignity contains three elements:

(i) Intrinsic value: This is the origin of a set of fundamental rights. It leads to the right to integrity, both physical and mental.
(ii) Autonomy: It denotes free will of an individual, which entitles them to pursue the ideals of living well and having a good life in their own ways. Autonomy requires fulfilment of conditions, such as (a) reason; (b) independence; and (c) choice.
(iii) Community value: It means the relationship of the individual with others, as well as with the world around him.

The meaning of the word 'Aadhaar' signifies 'foundation' or 'base'. It has become the most talked about issue, not only in India but in many other countries and international bodies as an exercise in defining what the contours of privacy are. One mention of the word and people associate with the largest human identification number scheme conceptualized by the government in early 2006. The scheme was launched in 2009 with enrolment processes starting in 2010. A special body known as the UIDAI was formulated. Under this scheme, the government issued identification cards to citizens which were unique to their identity.

As of July 2018, over 1.25 billion people have enrolled in Aadhaar, which represents 90 per cent of the total estimated population of the country. The huge success behind this scheme is due to the fact that no other identification document is as widely and commonly possessed by all citizens and most of the identity documents do not enjoy the quality of portability. UIDAI claims Aadhaar to be a 'unique identity' as it lends assurance and accuracy on account of existence of fake, bogus and ghost cards, vide process of duplication and authentication. UIDAI also claims that not only it is a foolproof method of identifying a person but also an instrument whereby a person can enter into any transaction without requiring any other document in support. It has become a symbol of digital economy and has enabled multiple avenues for the common man.

Initially, the Aadhaar scheme was not under any legislative umbrella. With an increase in the use of Aadhaar, it was found useful and, therefore, was decided to be backed by a parliamentary enactment. The Aadhaar (Targeted Delivery of Financial and Other Subsidies, Benefits and Services) Act, 2016, was passed by the legislature to administer the entire process.

Soon after, the Aadhaar scheme and the architecture built thereupon by the Aadhaar Act received scathing criticism from various sections of the society. According to them, Aadhaar invaded the Right to Privacy of every citizen and created a tendency to formulate a surveillance State, where each individual is kept under strict observation by designing their life profile and movement.

The constitutionality of the Aadhaar Act was challenged

for the first time in case of *Puttaswamy v. Union of India.* Even after Aadhaar had got a shield of statutory cover, the challenge persisted as the very enactment known as Aadhaar (Targeted Delivery of Financial and Other Subsidies, Benefits and Services) Act, 2016, was challenged as constitutionally impermissible. Two important issues were raised: first, whether the Aadhaar project creates a tendency to achieve a surveillance State; and second, whether the Aadhaar Act violates Right to Privacy, which is now recognized as a fundamental right.

With regards to the first issue, namely the grievous charge of creating a surveillance State, the court was of the opinion that the enrolment agency, which collects biometric and demographic details of individuals, is appointed either by UIDAI or by a Registrar (Section 2(s)). UIDAI is a unique body constituted under the Aadhaar Act, and the registrars are appointed through memorandum of understanding or agreements for enrolment, and are to abide by a code of conduct and processes, policies and guidelines issued by the authority. The registrars are prohibited from using the information collected for any purpose other than uploading the information to Central Identities Data Repository (CIDR).

The uploaded data is then encrypted and immediately captured. The decryption key lies solely with the UIDAI. Section 2(ze) of the Information Technology Act, 2000 (hereinafter referred to as 'the IT Act'), which defines 'secure systems', and Section 2(w) of the Act, which defines 'intermediaries', apply to the process. Authentication only becomes available through the Authentication Service Agency (ASA). They are regulated by the Aadhaar (Authentication) Regulations, 2016. Their roles and responsibilities are provided by Regulation 19 of the Authentication Regulations. They are to use certified devices. The equipment or software has to be duly registered with or approved or certified by the authority or agency. The systems and operations are audited by an information system auditor. The requesting entities pass the encrypted data to the CIDR through the ASA and the response (Yes/No authentication or e-KYC information) also takes the same route back. The server of the ASA has to perform basic compliance and completeness checks on the authentication data packet before forwarding it to the CIDR.

The Act also prohibits sharing and disclosure of core biometric data under Sections 8 and 29. Other identity information is shared with requesting entity (AUAs and KUAs) only for the limited purpose of authentication. The data is transferred from the requesting entity to the ASA to the CIDR in an encrypted manner through a leased line circuitry using secure protocols (Regulation 9 of the Authentication Regulations).

Even state governments and police forces cannot obtain the information contained in the CIDR or the authentication records, except in two situations contemplated by Section 33:

(i) When the district judge orders so after giving an opportunity of hearing to the authority (even in this situation core biometric information will not be shared); and
(ii) in the interest of national security, where a joint secretary or a superior officer of the Government of India specially authorizes, and in this case every direction is reviewed by an Oversight Committee chaired by the Cabinet Secretary.

For the second issue, which covers the violation of the Right to Privacy, it was contended that the citizen's right to informational privacy is violated by authentication under the Aadhaar Act inasmuch as the citizen is compelled to 'report' his actions to the State. Even where a person is availing a subsidy, benefit or service from the State under Section 7 of the Act, mandatory authentication through the Aadhaar platform (without an option to the citizen to use an alternative mode of identification) violated the right to informational privacy.

The court was of the opinion that an individual's rights and entitlements cannot be made dependent upon an invasion of their bodily integrity and their private information, which the individual may not be willing to share with the State. Hence, it was held to be against the constitutional morality contained in both Part III as well as Part IV of the Constitution of India.

TESTS TO OVERCOME

Further, with regard to protection of this fundamental right to privacy, several tests were laid down by the judiciary, which was held essential to overcome any violation by State or non-State actors. As Justice Nariman in *Puttaswamy v. Union of India* observed, 'When it comes to restrictions on this right, the drill of various Articles to which the right relates must be scrupulously followed.'

The nine-judge bench of the Supreme Court in *Puttaswamy v. Union of India* laid down the 'triple test', which needs to be satisfied for judging the permissible limits for invasion of privacy while testing the validity of any legislation. The following are the components of a triple test:

i) the existence of a law;
ii) a 'legitimate State interest'; and
iii) such law should pass the 'test of proportionality'.

The Aadhaar Act, along with its rules and regulations, was deemed to fulfil all three components. This included the presence of an existing law granting the State the authority to encroach upon personal liberty when it served the legitimate interest of the State, provided that such intrusion remained proportionate to the

State's interest. What it essentially means is that in cases where it is necessary for the State to track individuals for its security and integrity, it has the power to do so.

Privacy, being an important element of the principles of life, liberty, freedom and dignity shall always remain essential in exercising and realizing fundamental rights as enshrined under Part III of the Constitution of India. It has been considered by the court as an intrinsic part of the Right to Equality (Article 14), Free Speech and Expression (Article 19) and Freedom of Life and Liberty (Article 21). The court held that the scheme being a beneficial legislation does not infringe any existence of a law, legitimate State interest and test of proportionality.

Now that we understand and are more aware of the repercussions surrounding the Right to Privacy, I believe, the State as well as various multinational corporations and organizations will remain cautious of infringing on personal freedom of the individual.

Identities

2014 NALSA v. Union of India

In a landmark move towards inclusivity, Kochi Metro employed 23 transgender persons in 2017 and constructed gender-neutral bathrooms.

As human beings, we first learn to identify ourselves. Research shows that toddlers as young as two years of age identify themselves with and as a particular gender. Our gender identity is the foundation of our roles in society. The question, however, that we don't usually ask is: what exactly are the parameters of gender? Is gender an umbrella covering set of characteristics like what we wear, how long our hair is, whether our nails are painted or not and whether we have a fondness for lipstick? Somehow, this seems to stem from the way children are raised. Women are taught to be delicate, take delight in fashion and make-up and men are taught to be more interested in sports. Women have longer hair, dress differently and subscribe to different roles in the society such as caregivers and homemakers. The world around us, however, is full of contradictions to these set rules.

SHIVANI IS A BRAVEHEART

Let me preface this by saying that at the age I am, and with the kind of life I have led, I, as a child or even as a young woman, never really understood transgender people or what their lives have been like in a society which at the time was completely black and white. While I must admit this comes from privilege, I am trying to understand more and become more aware. Recently, a chance meeting and a discussion about a matter that was heard in the Delhi High Court piqued my interest in how transgender people see themselves. A very interesting judgment of the Delhi High Court in the case of *Shivani Bhatt v. State of NCT of Delhi* in 2015 starts as thus:

> Go not to the temple to light candles before the altar of God,
> First remove the darkness of sin, pride and ego, from your heart...
> Go not to the temple to bow down your head in prayer,
> First learn to bow in humility before your fellowmen.
> And apologise to those you have wronged.
> Go not to the temple to pray on bended knees,
> First bend down to lift someone who is down-trodden.
> And strengthen the young ones.
> Not crush them.
> Go not to the temple to ask for forgiveness for your sins,
> First forgive from your heart those who have hurt...
>
> —Rabindranath Tagore

Authored by Justice Siddharth Mridul, the judgment is about the returning of the passport of Shivvy, who was born Shivani Bhatt. The Delhi High Court addressed the issue involving Shivvy, who was brought back to India after his parents found out that he is trans and imprisoned him. It is not really the law that caught my attention here. It was the first line—'Shivani is a braveheart'.

To me, this statement exemplified how we have treated a class of society. Even as a young child learns the ways of the world, they are taught that there are specific male or female behaviour patterns and any deviation from these patterns is subject to ridicule. I've heard children as young as eight refer to their effeminate pals as *chakka,* a slur for the trans community, subjecting them to ridicule simply for not conforming to gender domains.

The story of Shivani Bhatt aka Shivvy, the transgender child of Indian origin who was brought to India on the pretext of meeting his grandparents and was then kept against his will and beaten, ostensibly to 'cure' him of his 'disease', sent ripples through the bar of the Delhi High Court. The quiet, precocious child was a student of neurobiology, an intelligent and hardworking student. His passport was confiscated by his parents. The case was given quietus when the High Court intervened and ordered the return of his passport and his ticket back to the US.

Life can often be difficult and dangerous for trans people, more so in societies like India. Shivvy is the child of parents of Indian origin and settled in the US. He was 19 at the time of this ordeal. When his parents found out that he was trans, they manipulated him into coming to India to try and 'cure' him. His parents kept him imprisoned in Agra and forcibly took away his green card and passport. He somehow contacted the NGO Nazariya, who helped him with legal counselling and shelter, and then helped him approach the High Court.

The case was typical of how our society handles these matters; even educated parents living in ostensibly broad-minded societies will often resort to violence or denial concerning such issues. As easy as it is to blame the parents for being narrow-minded, the approach is often not due to anger but out of concern for the child. Parents often resort to these methods because they believe the child will not be accepted by society. The trauma that society is capable of inflicting on such a child is unimaginable. This causes the parents to either become fearful or go into denial.

The case and incident became a hot topic of discussion in

the teeming canteens of the High Court and no one could seem to stop talking about it. It was strange, and I suddenly realized that in all my years of life and practice, I had not given this idea much thought. The concept of gender being solidified into two compartments—man and woman—is so ingrained in my generation that it was not only odd but extremely disconcerting to be faced with the idea of gender fluidity. I sometimes do believe, and I might confess rather grandiosely, that everyone has a purpose in life that we are automatically driven towards. For me, that purpose was the rights of women. I gravitated towards it because mine was a time when women needed a voice and I strived endlessly towards doing just that. This work gave me satisfaction because in the end, if I was successful, I would see the vindication in their eyes.

When I heard about Shivvy, it was the first time I was faced with the idea that I may have completely overlooked a very significant section of society. As a society, we seem to shun those who are different from us. The transgender people unfortunately has borne the brunt of that. They are often shunned by their biological families.

These are individuals whose gender identities do not pertain to their biological sex. Thus, transgender people encompass those people whose identity does not adhere to stereotypical gender norms.

Communities like kinnars, jogappas, sakhis, aradhis have been a part of our society and even mythology. It is obvious that we knew of their existence, and yet failed to acknowledge them.

Gender plurality has existed in our society for millennia; it has been recorded in our texts as various characters, the most famous of them being Shikhandi, who was born as Shikhandini, a woman, to King Drupada, as the reincarnation of Amba to enable to fight Bhishma.

As India moves towards a perceptible shift in governance and social attitudes, we as a nation need to take forward-looking steps and advance all our people. In a landmark move, the Supreme Court, in 2014, in the case of NALSA did just that. By taking the first step towards legalizing the existence of the transgender people, it has paved the way for their recognition by the society. The case of *National Legal Services Authority v. Union of India* was a PIL to secure the basic rights denied to transgender community. The most basic of which is recognition of the mere existence of the individual. Unfortunately, our society had, until then, functioned only within the confines of male and female genders. Our government forms had only two checkboxes and so did school admissions and other necessary applications. It was this judgment that for the first time recognized and legitimized the transgender people and was a long time coming.

The judgment was hailed as a tectonic shift in attitudes towards acceptance of alternate gender identities and was a potent indicator of how social perceptions have changed. Eloquently defined by J. Nariman in the case of Navtej Singh Johar, constitutional morality is 'the soul of the Constitution, which is to be found in the Preamble of the Constitution, which declares its ideals and aspirations, and is also to be found in Part III of the Constitution, particularly with respect to those provisions which assure the dignity of the individual.' The Supreme Court invoked this hallowed principle while reflecting upon the issue:

> TG [Transgender] Community comprises of Hijras, eunuchs, Kothis, Aravanis, Jogappas, Shiv-Shakthis etc. and they, as a group, have got a strong historical presence in our country in the Hindu mythology and other religious texts. The concept of tritiya prakrti or napunsaka has also been an integral part of Vedic and Puranic literatures. The word 'napunsaka'

has been used to denote absence of procreative capability.

[…]

Articles 15 and 16 sought to prohibit discrimination on the basis of sex, recognizing that sex discrimination is a historical fact and needs to be addressed. Constitution makers, it can be gathered, gave emphasis to the fundamental right against sex discrimination so as to prevent the direct or indirect attitude to treat people differently, for the reason of not being in conformity with stereotypical generalizations of binary genders. Both gender and biological attributes constitute distinct components of sex. Biological characteristics, of course, include genitals, chromosomes and secondary sexual features, but gender attributes include one's self image, the deep psychological or emotional sense of sexual identity and character. The discrimination on the ground of 'sex' under Articles 15 and 16, therefore, includes discrimination on the ground of gender identity. The expression 'sex' used in Articles 15 and 16 is not just limited to biological sex of male or female, but intended to include people who consider themselves to be neither male or female. TGs have been systematically denied the rights under Article15(2) that is not to be subjected to any disability, liability, restriction or condition in regard to access to public places. TGs have also not been afforded special provisions envisaged under Article 15(4) for the advancement of the socially and educationally backward classes (SEBC) of citizens, which they are, and hence legally entitled and eligible to get the benefits of SEBC. State is bound to take some affirmative action for their advancement so that the injustice done to them for centuries could be remedied. TGs are also entitled to enjoy economic, social, cultural and political rights without discrimination, because

> forms of discrimination on the ground of gender are violative of fundamental freedoms and human rights. TGs have also been denied rights under Article 16(2) and discriminated against in respect of employment or office under the State on the ground of sex. TGs are also entitled to reservation in the matter of appointment, as envisaged under Article 16(4) of the Constitution. State is bound to take affirmative action to give them due representation in public services.
>
> […]
>
> As we have pointed out above, our Constitution inheres liberal and substantive democracy with rule of law as an important and fundamental pillar. It has its own internal morality based on dignity and equality of all human beings. Rule of law demands protection of individual human rights. Such rights are to be guaranteed to each and every human being. These TGs, even though insignificant in numbers, are still human beings and therefore they have every right to enjoy their human rights.

The inherent ideals of our Constitution, enumerated by our founding fathers and the basis on which this country has been created and dreamt of have been enshrined in Part III of the Constitution. These are basic human rights, the ideals on which any civilized society is based and created, and the only way civil society has any chance of surviving. We as a country have promised these rights to our citizens, irrespective of any majoritarian attitudes, be it political, religious or communal.

The most powerful aspect of the *National Legal Services Authority v. Union of India* judgment has been its sincere attempt at understanding 'identity':

> Gender identity refers to each person's deeply felt internal and individual experience of gender, which may or may

> not correspond with the sex assigned at birth, including the personal sense of the body which may involve a freely chosen, modification of bodily appearance or functions by medical, surgical or other means and other expressions of gender, including dress, speech and mannerisms. Gender identity, therefore, refers to an individual's self-identification as a man, woman, transgender or other identified category.

The stories that we hear of transgender people are few and far between. In India, there is no rigid understanding of what it means to be trans. Indian society at large had continued its long relationship with the transgender people, despite its outlook. But the nature of the relationship deviated. Instead of being honoured, they were denied jobs and dismissed in mainstream society, forcing many to resort to sex work and begging.

While in these self-appointed families led by gurus, they are treated as brothers and sisters, protected, provided food and shelter, and taken care of both spiritually and physically, they face the health and security risks that come inherently from a life that can include begging and sex work.

Till very recently, being transgender was considered a mental illness, and even today, despite the declassification of being transgender as a mental illness, the hospitals that offer gender-affirming surgery require psychiatric assessment reports stating that the patient has gender dysphoria to start the procedure. The entire argument of gender as a mental identification falls flat when you ask a person to prove that they are psychiatrically stable enough to identify themselves. It belittles the basic human belief to self-identification. The prevailing opinion in the trans community is that the right to self-determination of gender is inviolable, and any affirmation or mental health evaluation is offensive and inconsiderate. Gender identity should not be an unwanted condition, it is simply a way of life for a percentage of our population and needs to be recognized and addressed as such.

In the end, change starts with sensitivity and empathy. A very heartening case is that of Jeeva M., who applied to the authorities for change of gender in his educational qualification certificates, as he identified as a man. After considerable trouble by the authorities, he approached the Karnataka High Court, who then directed the authorities to take a decision within two days. The High Court held: 'Transgender persons' right to decide their self-identified gender is also upheld and the Centre and State Governments are directed to grant legal recognition of their gender identity such as male, female or as transgender people.' I have read that Jeeva M. considered himself fortunate that his parents accepted him the way he is, and even agreed to pay for the gender affirming surgery.

On the legislative side, The Transgender Persons (Protection of Rights) Act became a law on 5 December 2019, which incorporates the judgment's seminal takeaway, the right to self-identification. The Act gives the powers to the trans community to self-identify and apply to the district magistrate for a certificate of identification. Another major takeaway from the Act is the decriminalization of begging by transgenders.

Until 2014, India's transgender community had no legal recognition. It was the NALSA judgment in April of that year that gave them the right to self-identification. It also made provisions for reservations for transgender people across government and private sectors. While the judgment did have its flaws, it was well-researched, diplomatic and acted as a ray of hope for the trans community. In contrast, the Transgender Persons (Protection of Rights) Act 2019 has brought rage and sorrow to the Indian trans community, because it proposed the establishment of a board of people to determine whether an individual is transgender or not based on their genitals and whether they have undergone gender-affirming surgery. It prompted nationwide protests by the trans community and trans rights activists.

While the judgment of the Supreme Court and The Transgender Persons (Protection of Rights) Act, 2019, is a step in the correct direction, a mere formalization of identity does not create the atmosphere we as a society are hoping to create. The issue of discrimination and ostracization of the trans community goes deeper than a mere acceptance of their gender identification.

There is a deeper need to change the attitudes of the society towards them. The root to freedom from oppressive patriarchal structures is and always will be education. An educated society, rational and accepting in nature is the answer to our nation and our society reversing the tyranny of the ages that people have been at the receiving end of.

This judgment is our country's hope for a more inclusive society and a step towards a gender-inclusive acceptance of human beings as human beings, irrespective of their identification.

Are Marriages Made in Heaven?

The Triple Talaq

'Of all the lawful acts, the most detestable to god is divorce.'

—Prophet Muhammad

Divorce: a word truly terrifying to the masses, at least in the kind of society I grew up in. Through the course of my career as a family law practitioner, I've often wondered about this word and what it encompasses. The truth is, divorce, however desirable in a situation, is ultimately an undesirable outcome. This one word has a completely distinct personality when it comes to emotion and practicability. Being a women's rights advocate, I do understand marital separation and the need for women to escape a violent or an abusive situation when marriages go sour. However, as a member of society, I do still see the way divorces are treated and the kind of insecurity and hardship it brings for women, even if they are independent and self-sufficient.

Marriage partnerships are fragile by their very nature. It is often repeated in our households—one needs to compromise in a marriage. The wisdom that was passed on to us by our mothers and grandmothers while growing up and during our lives as young brides is mostly geared towards compliance and submission. To my mind, there is both good and bad in it. I have seen situations blown out of proportion by men and women, which really need nothing more than a basic mediation, and I have seen women being tortured and traumatized, simply because that is what was taught to their husbands all their lives. Marriages are fragile and complicated. So much so that I do not know of one person who in their lifetime has not considered divorce. I once heard a High Court judge, frustrated with a divorce matter being presented, say, 'If it were up to me, I'd have divorced my wife a hundred times!' Shocking as it was, this was one of the most loving couples I knew, constantly travelling together, always with each other, and I've always known them as the perfect team.

The truth of the matter is, however forward or independent our society becomes, human relationships in their essence remain the same; some days we work hard at them, other days they come easy and some days, we just want to run away from them and dream of a life away from our partners. The feeling is not something only young angsty newly married couples experience, but is the same for those who have been married for many years. The fact that getting divorced is difficult, more often than not, is the reason that we all try a little harder to make it work. This seems to be true for most of our society and most of the couples that I know of at least.

When my daughter was very young, her essays about 'India' started with 'India is a diverse country, where a lot of religions live together in harmony'. We've always been proud that our motherland is home to several religions and religious traditions which co-exist peacefully. The problem arises when we transpose the right to follow a religion to our basic human rights, or in the case we are discussing, rights as a woman.

Our diverse, tolerant country has been plagued by various social evils, and in almost all religious sects, there have been rules and rituals that strip women of their autonomy and sometimes life. For instance, Sati for Hindu widows, and Triple Talaq for Muslim women.

Triple Talaq or *talaq-e-biddat*, instant divorce or *talaq-e-mughallazah* (irrevocable divorce), is a form of divorce used by Muslim communities in various countries, especially by the adherents of the Hanafi School of jurisprudence. The practice allows a man to simply say 'talaq, talaq, talaq' and be granted a divorce from his marriage. With the advent of technology and newer faster ways of communications, this 'social evil' had, surprisingly, also gone digital, and there were reports of husbands giving Triple Talaq to their wives over email or digital messaging services like WhatsApp. As a woman, I can only imagine what those women might have gone through. Imagine going to sleep married, and when you wake up the next day, there is a message on your phone and you are divorced. The life that you built, crumbled, and there are no consequences or remedies, except for the mercy or the large-heartedness that your former husband decides to show.

Muslim law, in its essence, is a very gender-equal law. However, over the centuries, it seems to have been interpreted rather haphazardly. A woman, once divorced, cannot be married to the same man. She has to go through a period of *iddat* for three months to determine if she is pregnant, and thereafter, she may marry another man. People were still using this form of divorce despite the fact that even if the husband admits to taking it back, there will still be a waiting period of at least six months before the husband can marry his former wife and only after she has married another man. It was this 1,400-year-old practice that was declared as 'unconstitutional' and 'not integral to religious practice' by the Supreme Court of India on 22 August 2017.

The movement against the draconian Triple Talaq practice in India was spearheaded by five brave women—Shayara Bano, Gulshan Parveen, Aafreen Rehman, Ishrat Jahan and Atiya Sabri, who petitioned India's Supreme Court against talaq-e-biddat or instant Triple Talaq, of which they had been victims. Despite multiple hardships from domestic violence to multiple forced abortions and relentless demands for dowry, nothing could break the spirit of these women as they finally won the war against a cruel and regressive practice.

It is a huge nod to the diversity and the integrity of India that the judgment delivered by a five-judge bench, consisted of five judges each of a different faith—a Hindu, a Muslim, a Parsi, a Sikh and a Christian. What was most surprising about this judgment was not the fact that it outlawed the practice, but that it outlawed the practice basing itself on the fact that 'Triple Talaq was not an essential part of religion'. It was not a judgment based on secular morality, but on essentiality of religious practice and its application in modern times. It was a huge bow to the versatility and the dynamism of the Indian social and religious fabric.

This inequitable inhuman method of divorcing one's wife is illegal in many Islamic countries, including the UAE, Iraq, Egypt, Morocco, the Philippines, Sudan, Jordan, Kuwait, Syria, Yemen, Pakistan and Bangladesh. Yet it had continued to be practised in India in the most barbaric ways. The judgment was a victory for Muslim women, lifting the spectre of this dangling sword from their heads.

No verse in the holy Quran gives authenticity to such a practice. The Quran lays down a three-tiered calibrated divorce, keeping in mind human frailties. Divorce cannot be pronounced in a single sitting and must be preceded by efforts of arbitration, mediation and reconciliation by mediators appointed by both sides, who must explore the possibility of reconciliation. It has to be pronounced before witnesses and over three sittings over a period of three months. These months are to allow the couple to reflect on their relationship and not come to a hasty conclusion.

The first two sittings give an opportunity to the estranged couple to reconsider their decision and, if possible, reconcile and resume their married relationship. Dissolution of marriage through divorce is the last option when all reconciliatory measures have failed. It has to be formalized within a specific time frame with the fulfilment of the conditions stipulated in the Quran.

The truth is that the concept of Triple Talaq is alien to Islam as it goes against the very spirit of the procedure of divorce laid down in the Quran. Prophet Muhammad, when he was informed about a man who pronounced talaq thrice at a time, was so enraged that he said, 'Are you playing with the book of Allah who is great and glorious while I am still among you?'

After the death of the Prophet, when the Arabs conquered Egypt, Persia, Syria and other States, they found women over there better in appearance in comparison with Arabian woman. Women from Syria and Egypt insisted that if they wanted to marry them, they should divorce their existing wives by pronouncing Triple Talaq in one sitting. And this condition was duly accepted by Arab men because they knew that in Islam divorce is only permissible twice in two separate periods of *tuhr* and pronouncing Triple Talaq in one sitting is void, un-Islamic and shall not be effective. The Arab men knew that in this way they could not only marry these women but also retain their wives. When it came to the knowledge of the second Caliph, Umar, he decreed to give validity of dissolution of marriage by Triple Talaq irrevocably. But, unfortunately, the Hanafi Jurists, the successor of Umar, declared the practice of Triple Talaq valid, granting it religious sanctions and making it a horrifying precedent.

Egypt in 1929 was the first country to adopt a modern perspective held by scholar Ibn Taymiyya (1268–1328) and theologian Ibn al-Qayyim (1292–1350), with regards to the personal laws on marriage and family. Both Ibn Taymiyya and Ibn al-Qayyim declared that repeating 'talaq' three times would only be considered as the first step in the overall three-step process of divorce.

In 1943, Abul A'la al-Maududi, the subcontinent's leading ideologue, also opined against instantaneous talaq or talaq-e-biddat: '[Triple Talaq] is an innovation and a sin leading to many legal complications. If people knew that triple divorce is superfluous and even a single talaq would dissolve the marriage, of course, leaving room for revocation during the next three months and remarriage thereafter, innumerable families could have been saved from disruption.'[1]

Pakistan's 1961 Muslim Family Laws ordinance abolished this practice and provided for an Arbitration Council to attempt reconciliation and a 90-day period for retraction. Talaq must be pronounced by a notice in writing and communicated to the council's chairman. The wife can stipulate for the right to divorce in her *nikahnama* or marriage contract (*talaq tafuriz*). Additionally, she has the right to dissolve the marriage *(khula)*. Recently Morocco's new Islamic Family Law was enacted with the full co-operation of religious scholars as well as the active participation of women. Every change in the law is justified—chapter and verse—from the Quran, and from the examples and traditions of the Prophet Muhammad.

---

[1]'Islamic Scholars: Triple Talaq an Unfortunate Act', *The Times of India*, 14 May 2017, https://tinyurl.com/yv4f5d6w. Accessed on 29 November 2023.

The issue of Triple Talaq in India had occupied the public consciousness for long—between 2015 to 2018, particularly. It had become entangled in the necessity and urgency of reform within the Muslim community. We were trapped in resolving a medieval question in the twenty-first century, one that even the otherwise regressive Islamic Republic of Pakistan had dispensed with.

The traces of these archaic practices go back to the nineteenth century, the century that saw the beginning of reforms and the emergence of early Indian reformers. This included, among others: Raja Ram Mohan Roy, who is most widely recognized for his efforts to abolish Sati; Syed Ahmad Khan, a prominent critic of the Islamic orthodoxy; and Govind Ranade, who campaigned for the rights of widows and against child marriage.

These reformists faced huge backlash from the conservative sections of their respective communities, including death threats and fatwas of excommunication. Despite such opposition, some of these reformers were successful—the British government was able to bring in legislations banning many Hindu oppressive and outdated social practices, such as Sati and child marriage.

Unfortunately, reform within Islam remained stunted despite aggressive campaigns by Syed Ahmad Khan and his modernist collaborators. His associate, Sayyid Mumtaz Ali, for instance, can be considered as one of the earliest defenders of women's equality. Ali authored *Huqooq-e-Niswan*, a book in which he used Quranic verses to advocate for equal rights for women. He championed causes such as women's education, and rejected purdah, polygamy and forced marriages—practices he considered unjust and injurious to women. In the nineteenth century, there were many social reformers among Muslims, who, like Ali, took progressive positions, and wrote and spoke with conviction about reform and gender justice within Islam. However, the orthodox sections—the many Ulemas and their large followings—remained averse to change. They remained antithetical to change and perceived any prospect of reform as a threat to Islam. From a global Islamic perspective, this was more likely a threat to these entrenched Muslims than to Islam.

Soon after Independence, the first elected government of India decided to bring about the famous Hindu Code Bill to replace the Hindu Personal Laws. The Bill was introduced in the Constituent Assembly on 9 April 1948, and met with huge uproar and controversy. The Bill was subsequently broken into three different Bills: a marriage Bill, an adoption and maintenance Bill, and a succession Bill. Jawaharlal Nehru succeeded in getting the Bill passed in Parliament, despite severe opposition from some senior members of his own government, including Rajendra Prasad, the first president of Independent India.

Many Hindu leaders accused Nehru of being blatantly partisan because he did not include Muslim Personal Laws as part of this reform. Nehru's commitment to secularism surely took a beating due to this ambiguity. Though, it can be argued that he was right to not take it up at the time, in order to reassure the Muslims who had decided to stay back in India that their faith was welcomed. Nehru and his government were up against a difficult political context—its election had followed unprecedented physical and mental violence. Perhaps Nehru and Ambedkar felt it safer to proceed with reforms in the Hindu Personal Laws at the time.

After the passing of the Hindu Code Bill, the personal laws in India had two major areas of application: the common Indian citizen and the Muslim community, whose laws were not subjected to any reform. In the decades that followed, the Congress as well as other progressive forces had many opportunities to make meaningful intervention, but failed to do so. The hindrance to legislation would likely have been minimal—the All India Muslim

Personal Law Board (AIMPLB), which later blocked any forward-looking reform, was not established until the early 1970s. Yet, the conservative forces within the Muslim community held sway, and political parties continued to walk on eggshells.

The frequent conflict between secular and religious authorities over the issue of the Uniform Civil Code eventually decreased until the 1985 Shah Bano Case. Bano was a 73-year-old woman who sought maintenance from her husband, Mohammed Ahmad Khan. He had divorced her after 40 years of marriage saying 'I divorce thee' three times and had denied her maintenance. She was initially granted maintenance by a local court in Indore, which was challenged by Khan, who himself was a lawyer, before the Supreme Court. Khan contended before the Supreme Court that he had fulfilled all his obligations under Islamic law. The five-member bench of the Supreme Court consisting of Chief Justice Chandrachud, Justice Venkatahramaiah, Justice Chinapappa Reddy, Justice Desai and Justice Mishra held that recourse under Section 125 of the Code of Criminal Procedure to approach the court for maintenance is open to every divorced wife irrespective of religion. The court observed that merely paying deferred dower at the time of divorce is not the conclusion. The husband is required to maintain not only the divorced wife but also the children born to them. The court even recommended that a Uniform Civil Code be set up.

This case soon became a nationwide political issue and a widely debated controversy. It was the era post the 1984 anti-Sikh riots, when minorities in India, including the Muslims, felt threatened with the need to safeguard their culture. The All India Muslim Personal Law Board defended the application of their laws and supported the conservative Muslims who accused the government of promoting Hindu dominance. The Code of Criminal Procedure was seen as a threat to the Muslim Personal

Laws. The Rajiv Gandhi government, which had initially supported the decision of the Supreme Court, lost the Assam State Assembly elections in December 1985 because of the endorsement. A wave in the Muslim community to gain full autonomy of their personal laws had begun. The Congress government, in order to appease the Muslim community, gave in to the demands of the orthodoxy and enacted The Muslim Women (Protection of Rights on Divorce) Act, which gave maintenance to Muslim women only for three months after divorce, in effect, nullifying the Supreme Court's progressive judgment granting Muslim women the right to maintenance after divorce.

Discouraged by the government's actions, Muslim women, who had been victimized and insulted, went to the AIMPLB for relief instead of going to the courts and to many Ulemas, expecting support against their oppressive husbands. Instead of receiving help, they found themselves being doubted and questioned on many counts.

∽

The 18 April 1996 rally towards Mantralaya in Bombay marked the first step towards protecting Muslim women's rights and was the commencement of the social justice movement against Triple Talaq. Muslim women were willing to speak out against gender injustice, and find ways to challenge structures of power and authority within the community and the State at multiple levels. These groups sought to promote equal citizenship rights pertaining to all fundamental rights mandated by the Constitution rather than focussing on changing personal laws to enhance their rights; this partly accounts for their success in mobilizing women from all religious backgrounds to fight for gender equality. For the first time, Muslim women groups had taken the lead and carried the momentum for change on their shoulders. Two networks were at the forefront of this process: the Bharatiya Muslim Mahila Andolan (BMMA) and the Bebaak Collective. Both have questioned the authority of the AIMPLB to speak for the Muslim community and women in particular.

In *Shamim Ara v. State of U.P. & Others* in 2002, the wife filed an application under Section 125 of the Code of Criminal Procedure demanding maintenance and complaining about cruelty to her and her children, and of desertion. In reply, her husband mercilessly said that he had divorced her earlier and therefore she was not entitled to maintenance. No evidence was provided regarding the statement of circumstances, no proof for reconciliation and no witness in support of the talaq. The family court rejected the wife's plea for maintenance. The wife appealed in Allahabad High Court and again failed to get any relief. The Supreme Court in its Special Leave Petition rejected the arbitrary Triple Talaq and held that the liability of the husband to maintain his wife shall not come to an end based on just mere communication that she has been divorced. Justice Lahoti further held that the talaq must be pronounced in support of Quranic injunction. The term 'pronounce' shall not be used as the meaning of dictionary it denotes, which is 'to utter formally, to declare, to proclaim, to articulate'.

In *Riaz Fatima v. Mohd Sharif*, the husband pleaded that wife is disentitled to maintenance since he had already divorced her. He also challenged the paternity of the child by alleging that his wife was of bad character. The husband also produced the copy of fatwa to prove the validity of the talaq. The magistrate court rejected the contention of the husband, and awarded maintenance to the wife and child. The Sessions Court set aside the order of maintenance. The Delhi High Court on appeal laid down the guidelines regarding the procedure of pronouncing Triple Talaq:

1. Divorce shall not be against the mandate of Holy Quran and must be for reasonable cause.
2. Burden of proof lies on husband to prove the proclamation of Triple Talaq in presence of witnesses or in writing. Till then, talaq will not be valid.
3. Prior to divorce, an attempt must be made for settlement/ conciliation by the husband.
4. The husband must show proof of payment of *meher* (dower).[2]

The court held that before a Muslim husband divorces his wife, he must fulfil all the pre-requisites in order to give validity to Triple Talaq pronounced by him. From the time of its judgment in Shamim Ara's case in 2002, the Indian judiciary has tried to set up a trend in conformity with the Quranic injunctions so that all possible measures were adopted for bringing reconciliation between the spouses before the Muslim husband pronounces talaq. Islamic law of talaq, as prescribed in the Quran, represents the modern breakdown theory of divorce and not Triple Talaq. It was emphasized by the late Justice Krishna Iyer in 1971, ex-judge of the Supreme Court, that:

> It is a popular fallacy that a Muslim male enjoys under the Quranic Law un-bridled authority to liquidate his marriage. The whole Quran expressly forbids a man to seek pretexts for divorcing his wife so long as she remains faithful and obedient to him, 'if they (namely women) obey you, then do not seek a way against them' (Quran IV: 34). [...] in the absence of serious reasons, no man can justify a divorce, either in the eyes of religion or the law. [...] The Prophet was

[2]Aeron, Kriti, *Triple Talaq–a Battle towards Gender Justice with Reference to Shayara Bano*, 5 March 2019, https://tinyurl.com/yp4hppab. Accessed on 30 November 2023.

> indeed never tired of expressing his abhorrence to divorce. However, the Muslim law as applied in India has taken a course contrary to the spirit of what the Holy Quran or the Holy Prophet laid down and the same misconception vitiates the law dealing with the wife's right to divorce.

The dilemma and agony of the population comprising Muslim women in the country, who for 65 years had lived with the mental insecurity that years of their marital alliance can be ended just by the utterance of three words, was settled by the Supreme Court in one of the most celebrated judgments of this decade—*Shayara Bano v. Union of India & Others* in 2017.

Shayara Bano is now one of the most famous Muslim women in India. In the span of just a couple of weeks, her life had become the subject of numerous articles, blog posts and other opinion pieces flooding different Indian media outlets. Her story is indeed a compelling one. Coming from a relatively poor background in Uttarakhand, she married Rizwan Ahmad in 2002 according to Muslim Personal Laws. However, the marriage was not a happy one and upon her account, she soon faced acts of cruelty on the part of her husband and his family, including persistent demands for extra dowry and being subjected to physical abuse, notably forced abortions. After sending her back to her relatives, Rizwan Ahmad finally divorced her by way of Triple Talaq in October 2015. She filed a writ petition before the Supreme Court seeking to strike down of the three practices—talaq-e-biddat, polygamy and *nikah-halala*—as unconstitutional, as they violated Articles 14, 15, 21, 25 of the Constitution of India. Nikah-halala is a practice where a divorced woman who wants to remarry her husband would have to marry and obtain divorce from a second husband before she can go back to her first husband. And polygamy is a practice that allows Muslim men to have more than one wife.

The Union of India and the women rights organizations Bebaak Collective and BMMA supported Ms Bano's plea that these practices are unconstitutional. The AIMPLB had argued that uncodified Muslim Personal Laws are not subject to constitutional judicial review and that these are essential practices of the Islamic religion and protected under Article 25 of the Constitution.

After accepting the Shayara Bano petition, the Supreme Court constituted a five-judge constitutional bench on 30 March 2017 consisting of former Chief Justice of India Justice J.S. Khehar, Justice Kurian Joseph, Justice Rohinton Nariman, Justice U.U. Lalit and Justice S. Abdul Nazeer. The first hearing was on 11 May 2017 and the matter was heard during the summer vacations of the Supreme Court. On 22 August 2017, the five-judge bench pronounced its decision declaring that the practice was unconstitutional by a 3:2 majority.

THE JUDGMENT AND VARIOUS OPINIONS

The judgment, delivered by a five-judge bench all of differing faiths, contained three differing opinions—all of which clarified categorically that they are dealing only with instant Triple Talaq, or talaq-e-biddat, and not the other two forms of divorces in Muslim Personal Laws: *talaq-e-ahsan* and *talaq-e-hasan*. The former is the most proper form of repudiation of marriage in Islam. The reason is twofold: first, there is possibility of revoking the pronouncement before expiry of the *iddat*, or waiting period after divorce; second, the words of talaq are to be uttered only once. Considered an evil, it is preferred that these words are not repeated. Talaq-e-hasan is also regarded to be the proper and approved form of talaq. In this form, too, there is a provision for revocation, but it is not considered the best form as the words of talaq are to be pronounced three times. The courts, however, have not ruled on these two forms.

Justice J.S. Khehar, former chief justice, who was one of two judges who upheld the constitutionality of the practice, quoted the Constituent Assembly debates on Articles 25 and 44, which refer to the freedom of religion and the need to lay down a Uniform Civil Code, respectively. Justice Khehar stated that personal laws are part of the freedom of religion, which courts are duty bound to protect. He further stated that personal laws are based on beliefs and are beyond judicial scrutiny. On the other hand, Justices Kurian Joseph, Rohington Nariman and U.U. Lalit, stating the majority view, observed: 'What is sinful under religion cannot be valid under law.'

They asserted that Triple Talaq may be a permissible practice but it is retrograde and unworthy. Justice Kurian Joseph added, 'What is held bad in the Holy Quran cannot be good in *Shariat* and, in that sense, what is bad in theology is bad in law as well.'

Justice Nariman and Justice Lalit said, 'Divorce breaks the marital tie fundamental to family life in Islam. Not only does it disrupt the marital tie between man and woman, but it has severe psychological and other repercussions on the children from such marriage.'

Though Justice Khehar's is a minority view, it opens up immense possibilities for a fresh debate on the Uniform Civil Code, as he emphasizes that personal laws are intrinsic to religions and are a matter of faith. If such a debate occurs—and it should—I hope we are able to devise a code with heterogeneity of our nation in mind, as opposed to a quick imposition of the view that benefits those in power, be it the government or the orthodoxy. In light of this judgment, we need to rise above competing fundamentalisms and push for progressive reforms in personal laws, which affect the lives of all Indian citizens.

In furtherance of this judgment, the government introduced, The Muslim Women (Protection of Rights on Marriage) Bill, 2019, in Parliament. The Bill defines talaq-e-biddat, instant Triple Talaq or any other form of similar talaq pronounced by the Muslim man dissolving marriage irrevocably as void, i.e. not enforceable by the law. The Bill had contemplated for criminalization with a term of imprisonment up to three years for anyone found practising it. After a long series of wrangles, the government's Bill finally cleared both houses of the Indian parliament and is now enacted as the law of the land. The law criminalizes the practice of talaq-e-biddat, rather than merely confirming that a divorce pronounced in this way is invalid. Any husband pronouncing Triple-Talaq, whether spoken, written or electronic, can be punished with a fine and a three-year jail term. Arrests can be made without a warrant and bail is given only at the discretion of a magistrate.

The Bebaak Collective, along with many other activists, signed a petition in late July 2019, condemning the new law for setting punishments for husbands. The collective argued that rather than empowering women, this law would make them vulnerable in other ways. If former husbands were jailed, it could prevent them from paying post-divorce maintenance, and divest wives and children of financial security. In turn, it could leave women at the mercy of hostile, vengeful matrimonial families. Questioning the government's motives, they declared the law 'not pro-women but anti-minority'.

On the other side, the BMMA welcomed the law arguing that criminal measures alone can cease talaq-e-biddat. Its leaders argued that their perspective is informed by their grassroots work on offering legal guidance to ordinary Muslim women. They claim that in the past two years since Triple Talaq has been declared invalid, dozens of recent victims of the practice have approached their offices each year for help. Some husbands, declaring themselves subject to Sharia Laws rather than court judgments, have continued the practice regardless. Vulnerable and uninformed wives have hardly been in a position to confute them.

It is painful and difficult to understand the plight of women who have been divorced by their husbands through this practice. As India is a country where most women are fully dependent on their husbands, the import of this legal pronouncement is even more significant. Trivial fights between husbands and wives take place in almost all societies in the world, but this doesn't mean that the husband should shirk away from the marital bond. Triple Talaq is always considered as a vagarious and whimsical act on part of the husband. The second Caliph, Umar, had never meant for it to be permanent practice. The practice of talaq-e-biddat violated the basic human right of women. A marriage is a sacred relationship and a gift of God. Even the Holy Quran doesn't approve of this form of talaq and has been declared as haram by some Jurists. The journey from Shah Bano to Shayara Bano determines various precedents in favor of Muslim women. These precedents now protect the fundamental rights of Muslim women and lays down a path of light for other classes. The judgment is a beacon of light not just for Muslim women, but all subsets of our society, who have been in some way or the other traumatized, whether in the name of religion, region, class, caste or gender.

The Man from Nowhere

Charles Sobhraj and Cases across Borders

'The healthy man does not torture others—generally it is the tortured who turn into torturers.'

—Carl Jung

A child without a State, rejected by the world and abandoned by his father at a young age—such was the early life of Hatchand Bhaonani Gurumukh Charles Sobhraj. He was born out of wedlock to an Indian father and a Vietnamese mother. It seems like his childhood was rather difficult with the parents being in a tumultuous relationship. Soon after his birth, his father, who at the time was a man struggling with a small tailoring business, left the mother and the child. With an absent father, Charles was a traumatized child, and he often ran away to his biological father who was then settled in Saigon with an Indian woman. Unfortunately, his biological father had no interest in him. His mother had married a French militaryman when Charles was around four years of age and lived in France at the time. Charles was a boy who didn't have an identity; he was Indian and Vietnamese, living with a French stepfather in a family that seemed to see him as a burden on their scarce resources.

The neglect that Charles faced in his early life led to his personality become more and more attention seeking and dark, culminating in antisocial behvaiour. He could have turned either way, but the feeling of displacement and his need for money to reach Saigon, to his father, seems to be crucial factors in his turn to crime.

Arrested on his second attempt at minor burglary, he was imprisoned in Poissy Prison near Paris. Paris is notorious for hardened criminals but the prison launched Charles on a trajectory that would eventually earn him the name of 'the serpent' and would make him a prominent name in the lists of the world's prolific serial killers. The prison became a ground for Charles to test out his skills at manipulation. He seems to have eventually learnt that he could get away with just about anything as long as he understood the human mind and mastered the ability to 'play' with it. Thus began his lifelong quest of learning about classics, history, philosophy, psychology and law.

The prison sentence was crucial to Charles, as this was where he became acquainted with Felix d'Escogne. Felix was a wealthy and impressionable young man who wanted to help the prisoners and was thus volunteering at the prison that Charles was captive at. Felix, it seems, was instantly enamored with Charles, helping him get a quick release from prison and even letting Charles stay at his house after the parole was granted. It was in the company of Felix that Charles made his first foray into the high society.

The handsome young Charles was able to charm anyone he came in contact with. He would impress and enchant the elites at the parties Felix took him to with his refined knowledge of politics, history, philosophy, literature and just about anything else under the sun. It seems like it was at these parties that Charles was scouting potential targets for a campaign of burglaries that he would commit at the houses of the Parisian elites. At one of these parties, he met his partner, a wealthy Parisian woman named Chantal. As dramatic as ever, a young Charles was arrested for evading the police in a stolen car on the night he proposed to her. He was sent back to Poissy for eight months, while a supportive Chantal waited for him. This unfortunate instance was nothing but a picture of what was yet to come for Chantal, as her undying affection and unwavering devotion to Charles would bring nothing but misery upon her.

Charles and Chantal were married upon his release. Soon after, facing mounting suspicion by French authorities, he and Chantal, who was pregnant at the time, left France for Asia to escape arrest. Furthermore, Asia represented an untapped treasure for the deceitful and cunning Charles, owing to its archaic legal systems and the rife corruption in the region. They travelled through Eastern Europe using fake documents and robbing people who befriended them. They arrived in Bombay around 1970 where Chantal gave birth to a baby girl, Usha.

During his travels, he had started doing what are called confidence scams, whether in the beach towns of Greece or on the hippie trails of Afghanistan. He would strike up conversations with travellers after eavesdropping on them, charming them and gaining their trust. A few days later, these people would realize that all of their valuables have gone missing, and Charles would escape. He knew exactly what to say and when to say it due to his deep and impeccable understanding of the human psyche. It's said that Charles, having studied Jung's book, had broken down quality traits different people possessed and could manipulate them using that knowledge. He was almost universally liked by the people he met. He used fake identities, often belonging to his victims, in numerous countries to avoid recognition by the authorities.

The couple made a good impression on the expatriate

community in India. At the same time, Charles resumed his criminal lifestyle by running a car theft and smuggling operation, the profits of which were ploughed into his growing gambling addiction. A botched armed robbery at a jewellery store in Hotel Ashoka in 1973 led to his arrest and imprisonment. Faking illness, he escaped with Chantal's help, but both were captured shortly after. Borrowing money from his father in Saigon to bail them out, they fled India for Afghanistan.

Charles had developed a penchant for escaping from prisons as even the most impenetrable prisons fell short in front of him. It's said, he escaped from supposedly impenetrable prisons instituted in different countries such as India, Afghanistan and Greece.

In Kabul, the couple resumed their habit of robbing tourists following the 'hippie trail.' Arrested once again, Charles escaped by pretending illness and drugging the hospital guard, then fleeing to Iran, leaving his family behind. Although still loyal to him, Chantal wanted to leave their criminal past behind. She returned to France vowing to never see him again.

On the run again, Charles financed his lifestyle by posing as a mysterious drug dealer to impress tourists and defrauding them once they let their guard down. In the spring of 1975, Charles met Marie-Andree Leclerc of French-Canadian descent in Kashmir. This would go on to be one of the defining relationships of his life. Charles was eventually joined by a young Indian named Ajay Chowdhury, a fellow criminal who became his lieutenant. Charles wanted to start a criminal 'family' of sorts, in the style of Charles Manson. This 'family' of Charles's continued to grow as more people joined, drawn in like moths to a flame after bearing witness to Charles's charisma and enigmatic personality.

Additionally, Charles started gathering followers by helping them out of difficult situations, indebting them to him while he actually was the very cause of their misery. In one case, he helped two former French policemen, Yannick and Jacques, recover their passports that he himself had stolen. A common ruse performed by Charles and his associates was that he would entice backpackers who felt somewhat lost in the mystical East to stay with him. He would put on the persona of a trustworthy friend and gain the favours of the lost travellers.

He is proficient in more than five languages, which helped him tremendously in making his victims feel safe and comfortable. He developed a modus vivendi where he would befriend travellers and invite them to his bungalow in Thailand. He would hold parties and create a facade of a travellers retreat, and after gaining their trust he would start to mix Kaopectate and Mogadon, two commonly available medications in Thailand, rendering his victims unable to function and in extreme pain. It was then that he would pretend to help nurse them, but in effect had them captive. It is believed that the ones who tried to leave were killed, taken in the middle of the night and left to rot on some lonely highway in the beautiful tropics. Their valuables would be taken and anyone who tried to enquire about them would meet the same 'killer serpent'.

While Charles was usually known for robbing and stealing in his early days, he soon transitioned into a serial killer. Charles and Chowdhury committed their first (known) murders in 1975. Most of the victims had spent some time with the 'family' before their deaths and, according to some investigators, were potential recruits who might have threatened to expose Charles. The first victim was a young woman from Seattle, Teresa Knowlton, who was found burnt, like many of Charles's other victims. She had travelled from Bangkok and was en route to Kathmandu, where she was to study Tibetan Buddhism at the Kopan Monastery. She had travelled to Thailand to meditate and to experience the Buddhist lifestyle. She met Charles, who allegedly offered to be her guide and to take her to Pattaya Beach, where her burnt body was later found. She was found drowned in a tidal pool in the Gulf of Thailand, near the town of Pattaya, wearing a flower-patterned bikini. Initially thought to be a suicide, it was only found after an autopsy and forensic evidence that someone had held her head underwater until she had drowned.

The next victim was a young nomadic Sephardic Jew named Vitali Hakim. Vitali was a Turkish competitor in the drug trade. He was found beaten, with his neck snapped, and his corpse doused with gasoline and set afire. In Bangkok, Charles strangled Hakim's French contact, Stephanie Parry.

Dutch students Henricus 'Henk' Bintanja, 29, and his fiancée Cornelia 'Cocky' Hemker, 25, were invited to Thailand after meeting Charles in Hong Kong. Just as he had done to Dominique, Charles poisoned them using strychnine and then nurtured them back to health to gain their obedience. As they recovered, Charles was visited by his previous victim, Hakim's French girlfriend, Charmayne Carrou. She had come to investigate her boyfriend's disappearance. The murders of the Dutch students were discussed in a Delhi High Court judgment concerned with extradition of Charles to Thailand. An extract from the judgment describing the circumstances surrounding the murders has been produced below:

> In the WANG NOI CASE the allegations against the fugitive offender are that on December 11, 1975, Mr. H. Bintanja and Miss Cocky Henken came to Thailand by air and both of them filled up disembarcation cards, that they would stay at Asia Hotel but they did not stay there. Instead, they stayed with Mr. Alian Gauthier, one Miss Marie Androe Larc and Mr. Ajay Chaudhary at Kanit apartment housed at Salabeeng Road, Bangkok in room No. 503. Both of them thereafter

were not seen coming out of their apartment for five days and were lying sick in room No. 503. It is further alleged that during this period Mr. Alian Gauthier prevented other persons from seeing or visiting Mr. H. Bintanja and Miss Cocky Henken so much so that even the cleaning of the room was prevented. During the night of December 15/16 of 1975 at about 00.02 hours Mr. Alian Gauthier and Mr. Ajay Chaudhary took Mr. H. Bintanja and Miss Cocky Henken out of the Kenit appartment by a motor car and by putting them on the back seat in a manner as if they were sleeping. On the following day i.e. 16th December, 1975 at about 00.09 hours Mr. Alian Gauthier and Mr. Ajay Chaudhary returned back, both of them had their legs splashed with mud from their shoes upto their knees and had with them a rubber hose with smell or oil. The daily newspaper on that day published the news of foreigners having been killed by soaking with oil and burning them. This incident took place by the side of Paholyothin Road, Wangnoi. The case, came to be investigated and it was revealed that Mr. Alian Gauthier and his accomplice murdered the two victims and fled from Thailand. The search made by the Thailand police at the room of Mr. Alian Gauthier at Kanit Appartment resulted in the discovery of belongings of both the victims. This was two days after the murder. Mr. Alian Gauthier and Miss Monique forged their victims' passport by taking out the photos of deceased and by replacing these with their own photographs and thereafter presenting the same to the Immigration Officials at Donmuang Airport and made their trip to Kathmandu, Nepal.[1]

[1]This extract is taken from *Charles Gurmukh Sobhraj v. Union of India*, 1985 SCC OnLine Del 420: ILR (1986) 1 Del 457: (1986) 29 DLT 410, p.459.

Fearing exposure, Charles and Chowdhury quickly hustled the couple out; their strangled and burnt bodies were found on 16 December 1975. Soon after, Carrou was found drowned in circumstances similar to Jennie's, i.e., wearing a flowered swimsuit. Although the murders of both women were not connected by investigations at the time, they would later earn Charles the nickname of 'The Bikini Killer.' This was because his usual victims were tourists that were backpacking around East Asia and various other parts of the world, who often wore bikinis.

On 18 December, the day the bodies of Bintanja and Hemker were identified, Charles and Leclerc entered Nepal using the couple's passports. There they met and murdered Canadian Laurent Ormond Carrière, 26, and Californian Connie Bronzich, 29. Charles and Leclerc returned to Thailand, making use of their dead victims' passports for their travels. Upon returning to Thailand, Charles discovered that his three French companions had started to suspect him. They had found documents belonging to the murder victims and fled to Paris after notifying local authorities.

Charles then went to Calcutta, where he murdered Israeli scholar Alan Aren Jacobs for his passport, and used it to move to Singapore with Leclerc and Chowdhury, then to India and—rather boldly—back to Bangkok in March 1976. Charles was tried for the offences he had committed against Mr Jacobs. However, his conviction was later set aside by an order of the Allahabad High Court, which was further upheld by a Supreme Court decision later.

The High Court recorded a finding that the prosecution had failed to conclusively establish that Sobhraj was the male foreigner who had accompanied Jacobs to Varanasi on 3 January 1976, stolen his passport and traveller's cheques and utilized the same for his ulterior purpose after tampering with them.

Therefore, Charles's appeal was allowed and the division bench of the Allahabad High Court rescinded the order of conviction and sentencing recorded against him by the Additional Sessions Judge, Varanasi.

The Supreme Court went through the evidence adduced during the trial and came to the conclusion that the decision of the High Court was not wrong or perverse so as to warrant disturbance. The decision of the High Court was thus upheld and the appeal was dismissed.

Herman Knippenberg, a Dutch diplomat was investigating the murder of the two Dutch backpackers, Bintanja and Hemker. He suspected Charles even though he did not know his real name. His investigation led him to Alain Gautier, an alias that Charles had been using at the time. Knippenberg started to build a case against him, partly with the help of Charles's neighbour. Given police permission to conduct his own search of Charles's apartment (an entire month after the suspect had left the country), Knippenberg found a great deal of evidence, such as victims' documents and poison-laced medicines. He accumulated evidence against Charles for decades, despite the lack of cooperation by law enforcement.

The murderous trio's next stop was in Malaysia, where Chowdhury was sent on a gem-stealing errand and disappeared after giving the jewels to Charles. No trace of him was ever found. It is widely believed that Charles murdered his former accomplice before leaving with Leclerc to sell the jewels in Geneva.

Soon, back in Asia, Charles started rebuilding his 'family'. He began in Bombay with two lost Western women named Barbara Sheryl Smith and Mary Ellen Eather. His devoted girlfriend Marie-Andrée Leclerc was still by his side. His next victim was Frenchman Jean-Luc Solomon, who unfortunately succumbed to the poison intended to incapacitate him during a robbery.

In July 1976, in New Delhi, Charles's temerity reached its zenith when he decided that he would rob a busload of French students that he had befriended. The three women in his 'family' had tricked a tour group of postgraduate French students into accepting them as guides. Charles then drugged them with pills, which he pretended were anti-dysentery medicines. However, things started going sideways in the most spectacular fashion for Charles when the drugs started acting too quickly and the students started falling unconscious at the Vikram Hotel in Delhi. However, three students quickly realized what was happening and overcame Charles, leading to his capture by the police. During interrogation, Barbara and Mary Ellen quickly cracked under pressure and confessed to everything. Charles was charged with the murder of Solomon, and all four were sent to Tihar Jail in New Delhi while awaiting a formal trial.

In a Delhi High Court decision concerning Charles's bail, the judge remarked that Charles was a hardened criminal who was likely to abscond after being granted bail. An extract from the concerned judgment is produced below:

> From the material placed before me, the petitioner appears to be a hardened criminal. He is not only an undertrial but a convict too. He allegedly masterminded the jail break and in a case of murder his release has been prohibited by the Supreme Court. I am told that he is wanted in some criminal cases in some other countries also. Besides, he is a foreigner with no roots in this country. It is because of all this that it was argued, and to my mind not without justification, that there was every likelihood of the petitioner absconding.[2]

[2]This extract is taken from *Charles Sobhraj v. State*, 1996 SCC OnLine Del 300 : (1996) 63 DLT 9: 1996 Cri LJ 3354, p.94.

What is odd about the Charles Sobhraj story is that it has still not ended. The mastermind criminal refused to let his tale end.

PRISON TRIAL IN INDIA

In the two years preceding the trial, Smith and Eather attempted suicide in their jail cells. Charles, like usual, had his way in life. He entered his jail with gemstones concealed in his body. He bribed his prison guards and lived a luxurious life within his jail cell. His trial was a spectacle for all to marvel at, hiring and firing lawyers, bringing in the paroled Andre to assist and going into hunger strikes to get his way.

The police officers assigned to Charles's case described him as impervious to questioning and investigation, no matter how long it was conducted for. In 1977, however, he was charged with culpable homicide not amounting to murder along with charges of drugging and robbery. He was sentenced to 12 years in prison. Leclerc was found guilty of drugging the French students but was later paroled and returned to Canada, when she developed ovarian cancer. She was still claiming her innocence and was reportedly still loyal to Charles when she died at her home in April 1984. She was 38.

Charles gamed the system in one of India's hardest jails to survive, the Tihar. His prison sentence in India was due to end before the 20-year Thai statute of limitations expired, ensuring his extradition and almost certain execution for murder in Thailand. He, therefore, found himself in need of a prolonged sentence in India.

The enigmatic Charles threw a party in his prison in 1986, on the occasion of his tenth year of imprisonment. Little did his guests know, how they were falling for his conspiracy to escape prison. The party guestlist included prison guards and fellow inmates, who were drugged with sleeping pills. Charles walked out of his cell. He was finally apprehended by the Mumbai Police in Goa at the O'Coquerio restaurant. His prison term was enhanced by the court by another 10 years, just as he had wished. Sobhraj allegedly hired a senior BJP leader as his lawyer before firing him for someone else. He sought to dispute his identity, stating that he was wrongly apprehended as Charles Sobhraj and was in fact someone else. My husband and father-in-law were counsels for the State. My personal intrigue for this story emerges from the threats received by my husband to recuse himself from the case, made by the man himself. As far as legends are concerned, he didn't come across as a very awe-inspiring one to me.

On 17 February 1997, a 52-year-old Charles was released with warrants, evidence and even witnesses against him long lost. Without any country to extradite him to, Indian authorities let him return to France. He had gained a mythic status among the general populous during his incarceration in India. His manipulation skills and enigmatic personality had elevated him to a household name, with people almost believing that he possessed superpowers in light of all the things he had managed to get away with. He had a plethora of female admirers outside jail, who were willing to do anything for him at a moment's notice. In fact, throughout his trial and prison sentence, women all over the world had started falling for him. Attraction of such kind to famous psychopaths and serial killers is not an uncommon phenomenon. In fact, it is so commonplace that psychologists have named it hybristophilia. In it, people experience attraction (often sexual in nature) towards individuals who have committed extraordinary crimes. It is also known as the 'Bonnie and Clyde Syndrome'.

CAPTURED IN NEPAL

Charles, after his release from Tihar Jail, went on to live in the suburbs of Paris, enjoying a comfortable retirement. He hired an agent and charged thousands of dollars for interviews and photographs. He reportedly charged an upwards of $15 million for a movie deal based on his life. Meanwhile, families of the victims and investigators such as Knippenberg despaired on seeing a mockery being made of justice.

Then, on 17 September 2003, Charles was unexpectedly spotted by a journalist in Kathmandu and quickly reported him to the local authorities. He was arrested two days later by Nepalese police in the casino of the Yak and Yeti hotel. On 20 August 2004, the Kathmandu District Court sentenced him to life imprisonment for the 1975 murders of Bronzich and Carrière. Knippenberg and Interpol painstackingly collected all the evidence against him.

Charles's motives for returning to Nepal remain unknown, although arrogance and need for attention likely played a part in it. He appealed the conviction claiming that he was sentenced without trial. In September, his lawyer announced that Charles's wife in France would file a case against the French government before the European Court of Human Rights, for refusing to provide him with any assistance. His conviction was confirmed in 2005 by Kathmandu's Court of Appeals.

LIFE AFTER CONVICTION

In late 2007, news media reported that Charles's lawyer had appealed to the then French president, Nicolas Sarkozy, for intervention with Nepal.

In 2008, Charles announced his engagement to Nihita Biswas,

the daughter of his Nepalese lawyer. On 7 July 2008, Charles, in a press release brought out by Nihita, claimed that he was never convicted of murder by any court and asked the media not to refer to him as a serial killer. Later, it was claimed that he married his fiancée on 9 October 2008, on the occasion of Bada Dashami, a Nepalese festival, in a much famed, but not publicized, wedding that took place in the jail itself.

On the following day, Nepalese jail authorities dismissed the claim of his marriage. They said that Nihita and her family had been permitted to practice a *tikka* ceremony along with the relatives of the other prisoners. They contended that this was not a part of wedding, but a part of the rituals of the Dashain festival, wherein elders put a vermilion mark on the foreheads of their younger siblings as a mark of blessing.

In July 2010, the Supreme Court of Nepal postponed the verdict on an appeal filed by Charles against a district court's ruling. It sentenced him to life imprisonment for the murder of American backpacker Connie Jo Bronzich in 1975. Charles had appealed against the district court's verdict in 2006, calling it unfair and accusing the judges of racism while handing out the sentence.

On 30 July 2010, the Nepal Supreme Court upheld the verdict issued by the district court in Kathmandu of a 20-year life term for the murder of US citizen Connie Jo Bronzich and another year plus a ₹2,000 fine for using a fake passport to travel. The seizure of all his properties was also ordered by the court. Nihita expressed dissatisfaction with the verdict. The 'judiciary is corrupt' was their claim, leading to them getting charged and convicted in contempt proceedings before the Hon'ble Court.

On 18 September 2014, Charles was convicted in the Bhaktapur District Court for the 1975 murder of Canadian tourist Laurent

Carrière. In 2018, Charles was in a critical condition and had been operated on multiple times. He had received several open-heart surgeries and was scheduled for more. As of December 2022, he remains in a Nepalese jail, aged 78 and in poor health.

Creative Criminals

Man is considered to be creative. Our societies are built in a way that they harness and reward the most creative and innovative member. There is an interesting link between creativity and criminal instincts and I try to explore this by delving into some of the infamous crime incidents.

CALCUTTA'S FIRST SERIAL MURDERESS[1]

I came across a fascinating story on a podcast called 'Khooni-the crimes of India'. The story was regarding the crimes of a Bengali girl named Troilokya during the pre-Independence era. What intrigued me about this story was the interesting link between creativity and criminal instincts. To understand this link, I jumped down the rabbit hole of the Internet to search everything about Troilokya.

Bengal was one of the pioneers when it came to crime periodicals. When the English were selling their 'penny dreadfuls', Bengal had their own homegrown crime periodical called the *Darogar Daptar*, where I found the story of Troilokya. Finally, I came to know that this story is supposedly the earliest recorded account of serial killing in Calcutta.

---

[1]For my research on this topic, Deepanjan Ghosh's article helped me a lot. See: Ghosh, Deepanjan, 'Sex Worker, Con-Woman, Serial Murderess: The Story of Troilokya, Who Terrorised Calcutta in 1800s', *Scroll.In*, 26 November 2018, https://tinyurl.com/3wnbjfvt. Accessed on 26 November 2023.

Troilokya, by most accounts, was a *Kulin* Brahmin. As was the norm at that time, a young Troilokya was married off to a much older man. As a young prepubescent girl, she continued to live with her parents even after the marriage, which was a custom in her community. She was said to have met her husband just once before he died.

We have all grown up hearing horror stories of what happened to widows at that time due to Sati practice. Perhaps, the evil practice of Sati was the easiest to endure because the widows were treated as untouchables, and were not allowed to wear coloured clothes and eat spices. They were not even allowed to cross the thresholds of other houses lest their shadows pollute the married women of those houses.

Many widows were also shunted out into the streets. The best life they could have hoped for was to be taken in by some other family, and live as housemaids. It was this last option that befell this girl very early on in life. After her husband's death, she was taken in by a *vaishnavite* woman, who then changed the course of her life. Troilokya, who was supposed to live a submissive life, transformed into a creature entirely the opposite.

The woman, who had taken in the young widow, turned out to be someone who was in the business of procuring young vulnerable girls for brothels. It was here, it seems, that Troilokya fell in love for the first time. There are varying accounts of this incident. One account says that once the news of her dalliance with a young man got out, they were forced to elope to Calcutta because it was unacceptable for a widow to have an affair. The other version says that they both wanted a better life, and hence, they left for Calcutta to live happily ever after. However, she suffered her second blow at life when the man who had promised her a second chance at life sold her to a brothel in Sonagacchi, the red-light district of Calcutta.

But the story takes an unexpected turn. Instead of being submissive, Troilokya dominated Sonagacchi. She was young and beautiful and was desired by everyone. Famous for her charm and candour, she started to earn increasing amounts of money, leading her to a life she had scarcely imagined as a simple village girl. A far cry from the life she would have led as a widow, she bought houses and mansions and all luxuries she could want including armed guards and servants. However, beauty fades, and so did hers. She started to get increasingly anxious about her future. She had everything she wanted, and once again was probably worrying that it would all be taken away from her, like it was when she was a child.

It was at this juncture of life that she met a man named Kali Babu, who became her lover. He was a widower and had a son named Hari. It was then that Troilokya finally acquired a semblance of what she desperately desired—a family. By most accounts, Kali Babu and Hari started living with her in her house.

Although she had acquired a family, it became a hurdle in her profession. The presence of her paramour was not well received by her clients thus decreasing an already dwindling clientele. Financially crippled, this made her more anxious about her future. And, as is most often seen with desperation, both Troilokya and Kali Babu turned to crime.

It began with small-scale crimes. They lured Calcutta's young rich to her house with the promise of sexual adventures, got them drunk, looted them and left them on the streets. The police used to mistake them as drunkards and would lock them up for the night. The added advantage of this method being that the clients would usually not report the robbery due to embarrassment. But this didn't work out for long. Soon, news of young men being robbed at Troilokya's brothel was out, and they could no longer lure fresh blood.

The next ruse was even more creative. They decided to exploit the marriage system. In the *Strotiya* Brahmins of Calcutta, the concept of dowry does not exist; instead, there is a custom of bride price. The father of the groom has to give substantial money and gifts to the father of the bride as a compensation for the bride. In the difficult marriage market of Bengal at that time, where girls were few and hard to come by, it meant that the father of the bride could ask for whatever price he wanted.

They would find families based outside Calcutta, who were desperate to find brides for their sons, and invite them to a rented house in a respectable district of Calcutta. It would be like a set from a play—with fake relatives, rented furniture and rented cousins. They would hire some young unknown girl to play the role of the bride and fix the match.

The marriage would take place with all pomp and show, and as soon as the bride's price was paid, she was dispatched to the husband's house along with some accomplices posing as maids according to the custom. After a month or two, after the gifts from the groom's family were received, she would ask to visit her parents. This seemingly innocent request was acceded too, and the bride and her accomplices decamped along with all the gold and jewellery. Troilokya would then pay off the actors and keep the rest of the money.

Eventually, this too had to end. People soon got suspicious. The woman, who was hired to play the role of the bride, no longer fit the role of a young nubile shy pre-teen. It was, again, time to innovate for Troilokya and Kali Babu. In ever increasing stages, they were turning to bigger crimes. The next nefarious crime they indulged in was human trafficking. They would kidnap young girls from wherever they could find and start selling them off as wives to desperate families looking for brides for their sons. However, the news of young women disappearing in and around

Calcutta spread like wildfire, and they had to abandon this idea.

Desperate, and increasingly running out of cons, they decided to commit the heinous crime of murdering a person. Kali Babu started to work for a rich man, whom he promised to procure jewellery for low prices. Then, he went to a jewellery store, selected some items, and asked for them to be sent to the address Kali Babu provided, promising that the money would be paid as soon as the jewellery was received. As usual, the address was of a rented apartment, and the shop assistant who had got the jewellery was murdered and buried under the floor of the apartment. Kali Babu, then took the jewellery to his employer and took the money he was given. However, Kali Babu's good days soon ended, when the case was handed over to inspector Mukhopadhyay, who has recorded his account in the *Darogar Daptar.* The inspector managed to find the rented accommodation and unearthed the body, and finally the decline of the murderous couple started.

After this incident, Kali Babu was hanged to death, but Troilokya managed to escape the clutches of judiciary. After sometime, Troilokya started to approach her ageing acquaintances in Sonagacchi who were going through the same problems. She promised them that they could double their jewellery and assets with holy Baba's blessings if they visited him dressed in their finery. She used to take them to an abandoned garden in Maniktala, Calcutta, and tell the women to bathe in a pond, where these gullible women were looted and drowned by the ageing and desperate Troilokya.

She was caught when a passerby caught her red-handed while she was trying to drown another woman. The victim and the passerby then took her to the police station, where, once again, she was inexplicably let go of. Although Mukhopadhyay continued to pursue the case, the policeman who had previously let her go, hindered and sabotaged the investigation.

After this debacle, Troilokya had to move to another house, which was a shared household. When she found out that another inhabitant, who lived in the same house, had considerable amount of gold, she tried to drug this woman, but failed. Then, Troilokya's desperation made her choke this woman, kill her and loot all the jewellery.

As luck would have had it, the case was investigated by Mukhopadhya, who understood the whole modus operandi as soon as he found out that Troilokya was living in the same house. He laid a trap and decided to arrest the only person in the world Troilokya cared for—Hari.

It was enough for her to confess. She was hanged. In an odd twist of fate, a woman considered being heartless and without any mercy, who had killed many, ruthlessly and relentlessly, gave herself up for her adopted son.

THE AMARENDRA PANDEY MURDER[2]

An article in *Time*, published in 6 August 1934, is the reason for me coming across this almost forgotten incident in our history.[3] Creativity in crime is fascinating to me, and so is the ingenuity of the police and the investigators who get hold of these criminals. This fascinating case from pre-Independence era is probably the first case of bio terrorism.

Amarendra Pandey was a 20-year-old co-heir to the extremely wealthy Pakur Estate. He and his half-brother Benoyendra Chandra Pandey were both sons of the Raja of Pakur and were heirs to his estates as well as the estates of Rani Surjabati Devi

---

[2]For researching on this topic, I referred to: Paul, Rudrajit, *Bacteria as a Murder Weapon: A Tale from Colonial Calcutta,* 2019.

[3]'Medicine: Black Death', *Time, 6 August* 1934, https://tinyurl.com/4u632dw8, Accessed on 26 November 2023.

of Deodhar. Pakur was a small but prosperous zamindari estate in Santhal Paragans of the present Jharkhand. In fact, it was one of the richest estates of Bengal at that time and this inheritance involved a large property and prestige. However, at the time of his father's death, Amarendra was a minor, making Benoyendra the sole custodian of the estate, who, according to popular gossip, and later, statements by his family members, led a dissolute life squandering the family riches. In 1931, Amarendra came of age and started to demand his share of wealth. It was then that Benoyendra became his enemy.

The story began with Amarendra and Rani Surjabati deciding to leave Calcutta after the auspicious Durga Puja. Amarendra's brother, Benoyendra, expressed his desire to go see Surabjati and Amarendra off at Howrah station. On the way to the platform, Amarendra was hit by someone who was described as a 'black man'. Amarendra was initially a little angry immediately after being jostled, because he felt as if someone had pricked him. Benoyendra tried to deflect the issue but Amarendra showed his arm and the prick mark, and sure enough there was a slight wound. Everyone then forgot about the incident; after all, how often does one really think about a pin prick.

When they reached Deoghar, relatives became more and more anxious about Amarendra and his failing health. Therefore, after three days of starting from Calcutta, they returned on 29 November, where Amarendra was examined by another doctor, who advised taking a blood culture.

Meanwhile, on 4 December 1933, Amarendra passed away suddenly. The cause of death was stated to be septic pneumonia, and the body was immediately cremated by the relatives at the Kalighat crematorium. The hurried manner of the cremation was suspicious. Still, given that the body had already been cremated, there was little anyone could do. However, it was later discovered, that the blood sample taken from Amarendra had cultured a bacterium that had not been heard of in Calcutta for the last five years. It was found that Amarendra's blood was infected with germs of bubonic plague. For many days, it was just whispers, because everyone was afraid of besmirching the name of a royal family. But eventually a petition was presented to the Deputy Commissioner of Police, Calcutta, on 22 January 1934 to initiate an investigation. The investigation was handed over to the illustrious Le Brocq and Sarat Chandra Mitra. Benoyendra was arrested after 24 days of the complaint being filed, on 16 February 1934, and the whole ball of wool finally unravelled.

As the investigations into the death of Amarendra Pandey progressed, one name kept cropping up, Dr Taranath. Taranath was initially referred to as a doctor. During investigations it was discovered that, Taranath, whose medical degree was dubious, was actually a laboratory assistant. He, through his work as a laboratory assistant, was familiar with the basic ideas of microbiology and had tried to obtain a sample of bacilli kept stored at Haffkine Institute for research in May 1932. His attempt however had failed as the laboratory refused to give a sample without any authorization.

Interestingly, that was not the first time an attempt on Amarendra Pandey's life had been made. It came to the knowledge of the investigative agencies that, earlier, there was an attempt to infect him with the tetanus bacteria by an infected pince-nez.

After failing to obtain the sample of the deadly bacteria, another plan was hatched. Taranath was placed as an assistant with Dr Ukil of Calcutta. After declaring that he had seemingly developed a cure for the deadly plague, he requested the good doctor to give him a reference letter claiming that he needed to test his cure against the live culture.

On 1 July, Benoyendra went again to Bombay and stopped

at the Sea View Hotel. On arrival, he made strenuous efforts, including offers of money, to obtain plague culture from Dr Nagrajan and Dr Sathe—two veterinary surgeons attached to the Haffkine Institute—but failed. Then, Benoyendra came to know that he could get plague culture at the Arthur Road Infectious Diseases Hospital. Thereupon, he saw Dr Patel, the superintendent of that hospital, and asked him to allow his doctor friend to work in his laboratory on his alleged cure. Eventually, Dr Patel was persuaded to accede to this request, and he instructed his assistant, Dr Mehta, that a Bengali doctor was coming to do some work on plague bacilli and to give him facilities.

At Benoyendra's request, Dr Mehta obtained Dr Patel's permission to indent for one tube of live plague culture from the Haffkine Institute until Dr Taranath arrived. There, Taranath showed as if he was working with the bacillus, and once he obtained a sizeable amount of culture, Benoyendra and Taranath together purchased rats in the market. On the evening of 12 July, when an experiment on one of the rats was still incomplete, Taranath told Dr Mehta that he had urgent work in Calcutta and must leave immediately. He asked him to convey his thanks to Dr Patel and said that he would return later on, but he never returned nor did he correspond with either Dr Patel or Dr Mehta. Benoyendra and Taranath left Bombay together that night for Calcutta. All of his actions were aided by Dr Sivapada Bhattacharya, whose reference letters aided Taranath in getting over many hurdles.

Dr Mehta saw no signs of any cure or medicine being applied by Taranath to the rats during the experiments. Apart from statements made by Benoyendra and Taranath, there is not a vestige of evidence to show that Taranath either had or thought he had at any time discovered a cure for plague, or wished to test it, or that Benoyendra had any other purpose in going to Bombay than either to procure plague culture, or to obtain for Taranath facilities which would enable to procure it. The practicability of removing culture from the Arthur Road Hospital, carrying it from Bombay to Calcutta and keeping it alive from July to December, was established beyond doubt by the medical evidence.

As Amarendra's death was the subject of police investigation, the medical evidence was again reviewed. Dr Santosh K. Gupta, of the Calcutta School of Tropical Medicine, examined the blood culture and reported 'suspicious bipolar rods.' He consulted with the professor of pathology, Captain Pasricha. The cultures were inoculated into a white rat, which died and postmortem examination of the rat revealed plague bacilli. Thus, the cause of death was established beyond doubt. The microbiological slides were submitted as evidence at the trial and the judges examined them under the microscope. Meanwhile, investigation was ongoing to find the perpetrators of the crime. Although many people suspected Benoyendra, it was not easy to link him to the crime. The affairs at Bombay, as mentioned earlier, were revealed much later through efforts of the family lawyer.

Benoyendra had travelled to Bombay earlier in 1932 and under a false pretense, tried to obtain plague bacilli. But the Haffkine Institute turned him down. This information was revealed by the family attorney, Mr Kalidas Gupta, with the help of a local guide in Mumbai named Ratan Salaria. Ratan was the all-purpose handyman for Benoyendra during his stay at Bombay. Kalidas Gupta was an astute lawyer, adept in digging up clues. It was he who also secretly met Balikabala, the mistress of Benoyendra, and found out that Benoyendra often met Taranath at her home. The name of Taranath in conjunction with the theft of plague bacilli from Bombay was already known to the police. This was thus, the first proven connection of Benoyendra with this nefarious scheme.

During the court hearings, Ashok Mitter came forward as

witness. He was a student who knew Amarendra. He said that he was present at Howrah Station on the day of the incident. After the fatal pin-prick, he had examined Amarendra's arm and found a puncture mark along with a drop of liquid on his sleeve.

Benoyendra admitted that he had been to Bombay to arrange for film work, but denied that Taranath had ever been with him to Bombay. Further, he said that he had never heard anything about Amarendra having been pricked at Howrah Station. While Taranath was out on bail, Gauri Sen, associated with the Medical Supply Concern where Taranath was employed as a bacteriologist, inquired about his involvement in the murder. Taranath replied that his actions were nothing compared to those who had done more and remain unpunished.

The accused, arrested in February 1934, were committed for trial in May, and were under trial until February 1935. Two of the accused were sentenced to death. The High Court modified the death sentence to transportation for life. Two things were instrumental in proving this murder. The investigation, where it was ascertained that Taranath and Benoyendra went to Mumbai to procure plague bacilli, and the fact that the plague bacilli was kept alive from July 1933 to November 1933.

When the country gained Independence in 1947, various political prisoners were released. Among them, Benoyendra also gained immunity and was released from jail. However, upon release, his mental condition was said to have been unstable. One day, armed with a gun, he locked himself up in a room and threatened to kill everyone present. A gunfight with the police ensued and he was eventually killed.

The case is fascinating because it is one of the first cases of bio-terrorism. The ingenuity employed by the accused is almost unthinkable and the meticulous thought and planning that went into this particular act is almost admirable.

KANKAL BARI CASE

This was a case reported in loud headlines in 2015. A man called Aurabindo De, 77 years old, had committed suicide by setting himself on fire. The newspapers had a field day reporting the case: they called it 'The House of Skeletons'.

I do not think I have the complexity of thought to imagine what had transpired to create these events. I can only put the facts as were reported, for the reader to see that all crime is not necessarily a product of a cruel or a greedy mind.

Aurabindo De was 77 when he committed suicide by setting himself on fire. He had returned to Calcutta from Bangalore in 1989 after retiring from his post of Director at Alfred Helbert India Limited. Aurabindo found out about Debjani's—his daughter—death in March 2015.

Partho De was Aurabindo's son and was nearly 18 years of age when he moved back to Calcutta along with his family in 1989. He lived abroad for a short span of time and held a degree in Engineering. He worked at a major IT company in Bangalore but quit his job after his mother's death to move back to his ancestral home in Kolkata.

At the time of his father's death, he had a filthy room with food littered all over the floor. Near his bed, a heap of bones was found by the police. These were the skeletons of the two labrador dogs previously owned by the De family along with the skeleton of his elder sister, Debjani De. There were stuffed toys placed near the skull. He had been living with the dead remains of his sister and the dogs for months.

Partho believed that after Debjani's demise, she would visit him at night. He also kept food for her, in hopes of bringing her back to life. He kept the remains of the dogs as he thought that they were the companions of his sister. Some of the things recovered from the house were drawing books with sketches of dogs and monkeys in various postures. According to news reports, it seemed as if a first standard student had drawn them.

Debjani was a music teacher at Don Bosco Convent School. After quitting her job, she, along with the De family, would live off of rents given by the tenants till 2014. The family also owned two dogs who died one after the other in August 2014. Debjani was very fond of them, and their demise turned out to be a major emotional trigger for her. She was convinced that the house was full of negative energy, and hence she decided to cleanse its aura by fasting. She wouldn't eat for days, which extended to weeks and then to months, and she eventually passed away due to starvation.

Shanti De was the wife of Aurabindo De and the mother of Debjani and Partho De. She was suffering from cancer and passed away in the early 2000s. Partho's journals suggested that Shanti Devi was an abusive lady, kept the family on a tight leash and never let them mingle with outsiders. He has also mentioned how she made Debjani strip as a punishment for trying to be more independent. Shanti Devi thought that Partho was sexually incompetent and hence tried to send their domestic help to his room.

This incident possibly took place on 10 July 2015 at House No. 3, Robinson Street, South Kolkata. The house was jointly owned by two brothers, Aurabindo De and Arun De. The property was purchased by their father in the 1950s. On 10 July 2015, the neighbours to the De family noticed a thick smoke emerging from the window of the De Family's home and immediately informed the Shakespeare Sarani Police Station.

When the police arrived, they found that Aurabindo De had set himself on fire in his washroom. His charred remains were found in the bathtub along with a suicide note.

The police immediately detained Aurabindo's 44-year-old son, Partho De, who was present in the house at the time of the incident. Partho's behaviour was considered suspicious and erratic.

On 11 July 2015, Partho was brought in for questioning at the Shakespeare Sarani Police Station where he stated: 'I may have committed what may be a crime in the eyes of law but I did it because I loved them, my sister and the dogs, and I couldn't let them go.'[4]

The police were stunned at this new discovery and went back to the house for further investigation. Upon reaching, they heard the voice of Joyce Meyer, a popular Christian motivational speaker, coming from Partho De's bedroom which would play in-loop on the speakers in the De House all day long.

Partho's room was extremely untidy and unclean, with a heap of bones kept near his bed. A cot was also recovered from the room which had a fully clothed skeleton of his elder sister, Debjani De. Her skeleton was covered with a piece of cloth and a stuffed toy was kept near the skull. According to the forensic reports, Debjani passed away in December 2014 due to natural causes.

Upon further investigation, the police came across a bag of skeletons of the two labrador dogs owned by the De family and a skeleton of Partho's sister. A preliminary report issued by the SSKM Hospital in Kolkata revealed that no chemical had been used to preserve the skeletons. However, surprisingly, neither the neighbours nor people visiting the house occasionally had smelled a stench. Some news reports also stated that Partha De had thrown a birthday party in April and had a gaggle of relatives over. No one got a hint that there were rotting corpses in a room in the house. A security guard used to bring food for the De

---

[4]Banerjie, Monideepa, 'Kolkata's House of Horror: The Full Story', *NDTV.Com*, 11 June 2015, https://tinyurl.com/26pyj6fe. Accessed on 27 November 2023.

Family thrice a day, but he didn't find anything suspicious either.[5]

Kolkata Police also found several journals belonging to Partho De which revealed the dysfunctionality of the De family and suggested a possible incestuous relationship between the two siblings. The journal mentioned his deepest feelings and snippets about his upbringing and childhood days. Police had also come across several writings of Aurabindo till 15 April, where he mentioned his plan to divide the property equally between Debjani and Partho. However, the police wondered why he would consider leaving Debjani a share if Partho had told him about her death on 12 March. It seemed that the members of the De Family would only communicate with each other using notes, and not through verbal conver Sations.

Partho was probably charged under Sections 268, 269 and 176 of IPC along with necrophilia. He was also supposedly charged under Section 304A of the IPC. Partho was charged with public nuisance by the police for keeping three rotting corpses in his house and not informing public authorities about them and was sent to Pavlov Hospital for the mentally disturbed but he later requested to go to Mother House to continue his treatment. A few police officers who came into contact with De described him as a sensitive soul who could sing Tagore's songs.

Partho De was diagnosed with schizophrenia at the Pavlov Hospital. There is a good possibility that the journals were just a rambling of his delusional self. However, his doctors refused to believe that he was a necrophiliac.

He had a difficult childhood which impacted his mental health at large. He wasn't a dangerous man, just a delusional one. He had nothing to do with the death of his family members

---

[5]'Horror House on Robinson Street: Hidden Notes, Strange Sex Stories Emerge from Kolkata Police Probe', *Firstpost*, 17 June 2015, https://tinyurl.com/3vyz8mey. Accessed on 27 November 2023.

and was never charged for the same.

Although the statements made by him along with the timeline given cannot be fully relied upon, he was probably a firm believer in reincarnation and deeply loved his family. After recovering and coming back from completing his time at the hospital, he moved into a new flat. However, on 21 February 2017, Partho De committed suicide in a similar manner as his father. A possible reason for this could be the defamation he had faced by the media and the public at large.

Index